desire, high heels, red wine

Timothy Archer • Sky Gilbert
Sonja Mills • Margaret Webb

Foreword by Sue Golding
Edited by Mike O'Connor

INSOMNIAC PRESS

Copyright © 1995 Insomniac Press

All rights reserved.

Editor
Mike O'Connor

Copy editors
Phlip Arima
Lloyd Davis
Waheeda Harris

Canadian Cataloguing in Publication Data

Main entry under title:

Desire, high heels, red wine

ISBN 1-895837-26-X

1. Gays' writing, Canadian (English).* 2. Short stories, Canadian (English).* 3. Canadian fiction (English) - 20th century.* 4. Canadian poetry (English) - 20th century.* 5. Homosexuality - Literary collections. I. O'Connor, Mike, 1968-   .

PS8237.H65D47 1995   C810.8'0353   C95-930200-X
PR9194.52.H65D47 1995

Printed and bound in Canada

A number of Margaret Webb's poems in this collection first appeared in *Tessera, Descant, Matrix, Fireweed* and *Contemporary Verse 2*, as well as a chapbook entitled *When All She Intended was Blue Sky* by Gargoyle Press.

Insomniac Press
378 Delaware Avenue
Toronto, Ontario, Canada
M6H 2T8

foreword

The sly, the splattered, the wild, the bent; the bored, the sadist, the muscular; the tinge of mutilated corpse; the scarred, the Polaroid, the French whore, the boy; the whale and the ill; the classifieds, the cock-tease, the worries, the flab; the carrying on, and over and under and out; the bereft and the joke and the piercings and pain; pyjamas and drag queens and spunk and a needle; swollen egos, and clit-hoods, and dandys, and dens; the asshole awaiting in fits and throbs; the obnoxious as insight, the gossip as truth...

This is an uncensored volume of queer-style poetics venting sexual curiosities once mostly considered (and not so very long ago) illegal, demented or just plain wrong. But more than that, too, it's a strange little stock-taking of our predatory illusions, a rummaging-through of our collective trash in pursuit of new playtimes and night times and dead times; or, dare we now say it, of multiple-self times. For Sonja Mills, Sky Gilbert, Timothy Archer and Margaret Webb are remembering our memories, and with them, our mutating skins, in the strongest sense of the word: to remember; that is to say, to re-stick together, to re-package, to re-play. To wit: to re-member and therewith recreate a 'something' more fluid and slimy than that old standard-bearer, that one dimensional shell-game, that straight-jacket identity called lesbian or gay.

Laid before us are hand-picked souvenirs — at times rather terrifying, at other times, banal — forever rocking forwards and back to produce, in that (twisted) paradox of sexual technique, of fetish and make-believe, a kind of bizarre metamorphosis; a kind of metamorphic braiding of mucky-wet structures and mutating contents; a beat, beat, beating whose rhythmic gasps form the very basis of the story of our multiple lives. Or, to say the same thing, though in a slightly queerer manner: we have before us an 'us' which is no more nor less than a whole (truncated) host of sublime collages with no real morals, no morals to the stories — just collages of insistence, persistence, and play based on sex-time as real-time (or even as post-time), continually re-membering our multi-micro body selves.

In the wake of all these pleasured whimsies, elasticity and decay, a curious aesthetics has begun to take shape. Neither smaller nor grander than the moulting skins of our memories, it is one that re-claims the smelly body, its (w)hole and its parts, including all its orgasmic imperfections, warped though they might be. Baudrilliard and company, step aside! These queer, unnatural poetics reject outright a "body without organs" utopia. For the moment of otherness, not to mention fun, is not the (virtual or otherwise) surpassing of the body and its parts; it is the body, with all its dirty little parts.

And therein lies the tale.

Sue Golding,
London, England,
January 1995

Sue Golding, writer, director and philosophicus wanderus. She has been working with and against avant-garde, gay/lesbo theatre for well over a decade in the U.K. and Canada; has been, since 1984 president of the wild, absurd, and very queer, Buddies in Bad Times (Canada); has written numerous non-fiction and fictional works ranging from aesthetics to ethics to the glories of glory holes. Her migratory interests range from de Sade to Burroughs, Dada to Pop and back again.

Thicker Skin in Thirty Minutes
written by Sonja Mills
designed by Mike O'Connor
7

From the True Confessions of Lana Turner as Told by Her Movies
written by Sky Gilbert
designed by Andy Parks
21

Closure
written by Timothy Archer
designed by Mike O'Connor
47

Memories of Beef
written by Margaret Webb
designed by Peter Mansour
71

– for deb

sonja mills

thicker skin in thirty minutes

designed by
ike o'connor

8 — sonja mills

Wanted

There are several openings in my life. Applications are now being accepted for the following positions:

A fuck-buddy is required to replace my current fuck-buddy who keeps leaving bite marks on my bum. You must be available on short notice and be willing to scram upon completion of each project. Experience, strong forearms, an aloof demeanour and no particular fondness for any form of foreplay are necessary requirements for this freelance position. Although a friendly social rapport will be maintained for appearances, telephone contact will be limited to arranging sex. Applications for this position are accepted every day of the year except New Year's Eve and the 20th of February and are kept on file indefinitely.

The position of fuck-friend, an entirely different job than fuck-buddy, is always available. The job description is long, complex, and not entirely stress-free. However, both the pay and the benefits package are substantial. I'll like you, need you, possibly love you, but you'll still have to scram after sex. Unfortunately — among you, my friends, my fuck-buddies and my lovers — you will be the one most likely to be expected to deal with my pre-, peri- and post-menstrual mood swings and occasional suicidal tendencies. Unlimited long and short-term contracts are available.

Oh, and... (God, someone stop me)... I'm looking, also, for someone to fall in love with. This miserable, mutually masochistic and hellish position is available sporadically. The pay is lousy. Applicants are strongly urged to possess one or more qualities which are likely to drive me completely insane. For example, applicants who are involved in an exclusive relationship with someone else and/or sexually confused and/or uncommunicative and/or have no intention of working a day in their lives are most likely to be considered for this position. Pathetic, egomaniacal, self-absorbed losers are especially encouraged to apply. This is a three to four month contract position. Upon termination, your severance package will include grief, guilt, several weeks of desperate middle-of-the-night phone calls and a VCR.

To be considered for any or all of these positions, apply within.

Thank you.

A Winter Scene

The girl and I come home from a long night of grinding our cunts together on a dance floor (well, we have to go out and be sociable sometimes). We've had the first major snowfall of the winter — four inches of good, wet packing snow. We romp and play in it like puppies walking down the street from the subway and when we get to the house, decide to build a snow-dyke on the front lawn.

We name her Lou: a truck-driving snow-bitch with big tits and a moustache. And as the girl is finishing up — leaned over, attaching a rolled-up ring of foil from her cigarette package through our snow-mama's left nipple — I pelt her ass with a snowball. Her reaction is more severe than I expected. She tackles me and rolls with me through the wet muck, pulling at my clothes, grabbing my tits and telling me she wants to fuck me right here in front of all the neighbours.

I laugh and put my hands on the sides of her head. I want to pull her face close to mine so I can kiss her; but with an evil smirk she shovels a handful of snow down my pants. It's so cold I squeal and piss myself a little...

She notices.

Avijk

My best friend is Avijk the whale. He's a blue whale who lives in the ocean off the coast of Greenland. We talk on the phone. He doesn't really have a phone — it's a psychic thing.

My friends, lovers and family accept my relationship with this whale although they do not understand it. I don't expect anyone to.

In the past there have been newspaper articles written about our friendship and I've been more than happy to talk to the reporters because I want everyone to know how wise and loving my friend Avijk is. But the articles just end up making me look stupid or insane and people lose interest soon afterward anyway.

Avijk calls me when he's in trouble and I go and visit him. Luckily, the subway goes to Greenland — it's the second-last stop north on the Yonge line. He calls one day and asks me to come because he just killed someone. One of the local whales wandered away from the village one morning, got harpooned in the head, went crazy, and started hurting himself and other whales. So Avijk had to kill him. So, of course, I went up to support him through it — to let him know he had no choice — that he did the right thing.

When I visit Avijk, he doesn't need to actually see me, because his telepathic abilities are immense; but he knows that because I'm only human, I need a certain amount of physical contact in order to communicate completely with him. So he comes in as close to shore as he can and I take a little rowboat out to meet him so I can see him and touch him.

The next time Avijk calls, he's upset because he's breaking up with his lover. And it turns out he's a she and she's a lesbian. I hadn't known that before. Our friendship had always been so deep and spiritual that it transcended mere things like gender and sexual preference.

So, I go up to meet Avijk. She's really depressed. Her girlfriend is leaving her — packing her things as we speak — and Avijk asks me if I'll come down to her apartment in the ocean and talk some sense into her. Avijk waits outside while I go in — and it turns out her girlfriend is a bitch. A lying, cheating, selfish sloppy-cunt little bitch whale. And Avijk doesn't see the obvious because she's too much in love. We go to a seedy little bar on the ocean floor for some drinks, several actually, and Avijk finally starts coming around to seeing the bitch-whale for what she really is. "Yeah — I need a real whale. Not just some big tuna who's gonna fuck me around."

The third time Avijk phones, my roommate answers. The line is dead, so she knows it's Avijk and calls for me. But the line is dead for me too. I know she's there but I can't hear her. Something is terribly wrong. I leave immediately to go and see her — taking my boat out to the spot where we usually meet. Finally, she comes. Moving so slowly. She's very sick — dying. I cry, embrace her, stroke her. She cries a little, too. We say our goodbyes, and I go home feeling very sad.

I sit alone in my living room. I can feel something coming but I don't know what it is. I close my eyes — and for a moment, just a moment — I'm five years old. My grandmother is making Danish pancakes for me in the kitchen of her tiny apartment in Copenhagen. Suddenly, a tremendous force pushes open the kitchen shutters, reaches me in the next room and slams me, pinning me against the wall.

It's Avijk.

Avijk has died and her spirit has come here, faster than the subway, faster than the wind, and entered me. And I am filled with such tremendous joy and peace that I can barely contain it in my body.

My First S&M Experience

Laura-Lee McFarland and I were 10 years old in grade four. Best friends; we spent every day together, and I would sleep over at her house every weekend. Her house was better than my house, because she didn't have brothers or sisters and she had her own TV in her bedroom in the basement two whole floors away from her parents, so they couldn't hear us. We would drink whole big bottles of ginger-ale, eat potato chips and watch the baby blue movies that came on late at night. We watched women sucking on guys' dinks and tried to see how it would feel by sucking on each others' fingers. I could almost get her whole hand in my mouth, but not quite.

One of our favourite games was to sneak into the garage when her parents were sleeping, beat the fuck out of each other with her dad's tools then crawl back into her bed and push each other's bruises all night.

One hot summer night in the garage, we had nothing but our pyjama bottoms on; two smooth, skinny, flat-chested girls. Laura-Lee hit my arm with something we hadn't tried before — a flat wooden carpenter's ruler. The pain was different than when she hit me with hammers or wrenches.

It hurt more I think — but it was sweeter. She liked it too. Liked the way it sounded and the way my skin welted a bit where she hit it.

She asked if I wanted to play cowboys and indians. I liked that game a lot. She tied my hands together with rope as usual, threw it up over one of the rafters and while I stood on my toes and reached up as high as I could; she pulled the rope tight and tied it to the garage door, so I was sort of half-hanging, half-standing on my toes. I can't remember why we called that game cowboys and indians.

She hit me again with the ruler across my arms and shoulders and back. Hard. Each smack harder and sweeter until I flinched and yelled a bit without knowing it. She shushed me — "don't wake up my parents."

Then, without warning — that little girl pulled my pyjama bottoms down around my ankles and started hitting my bum and the backs of my legs and I got that funny weird feeling in my little, hairless cunt that I sometimes got when I slept at her house. I didn't know what to do when I got that feeling in my cunt. Sometimes I still don't.

When she was finished she wanted us to go in and get some pop — but I told her to go ahead and just bring some out. She was gone for a long time it seemed, and I just hung there — feeling the time pass, feeling every inch of my stinging flesh — and liking it, and not liking it, and then liking it again. And something else. Something I hadn't felt before. Left alone, hanging, stinging, exposed, pants down around my ankles and not a thing I could do about it... I felt something I knew I was going to want to feel again — I was humiliated.

And I don't know, but maybe if I hadn't played these games in the fourth grade with Laura-Lee McFarland, maybe I wouldn't understand why pain and why humiliation — can be so provocative.

A Conversation

a   Sodomy equals AIDS equals straight to hell.
b   What?
a   Sodomy equals AIDS equals straight to hell. Scribbled on that Walk For Life poster over there. And almost every word is spelled wrong.
b   Of course. It's no coincidence that hateful people are often illiterate or stupid.
a   And religious zealots are often hateful. That's no coincidence either.
b   Did I tell you that on my way home from New York I heard this crazy Christian fanatic on the radio going on about how he had proved that God condemns abortion? Same guy that proved that AIDS is God's retribution for homosexuality. Now he's proven that God's got it out for abortionists.
a   Oh really?
b   Yes, because several abortion clinics were affected by the earthquakes in Los Angeles ... 13, I think he said, were affected by the

quakes. That was his proof.

a   Did he happen to mention how many churches were similarly affected?

b   No, oddly enough, he didn't mention anything about that.

a   Fucking zealots. I'd like to just wipe them all out. Zealots and Nazis.

b   And cockroaches. Don't forget about cockroaches.

a   Yes, cockroaches too. I love you.

b   And I love you. But you know what I've always wondered? How can we be so sure that we're right and they're wrong? It's just a question, you understand. I'm not questioning my standards of political and ethical correctness. But, perception is a tricky thing. We're convinced that we're fighting the good fight, and the crazies are just crazy; but zealots are just as convinced that we're sinners, whatever that means, and Nazis are just as convinced that they're the chosen race, whatever that means. How can we be so sure that our perception of right and wrong is any more valid than theirs? How can we be so sure that we're "us" and they're "them"? Isn't that sort of egomaniacal? Isn't that just as intolerant? Are we bigots too?

a   Zealots, Nazis, cockroaches, and psych majors, wipe them all out.

b   You know what I mean. OK, never mind about perception for a minute. What about action? We know that homosexuality isn't just OK, it's fabulous. We know that abortion should be a woman's choice. We know that racism and sexism are ignorant. But to what lengths do we go to combat our opponents? Do we trash the homes of known white supremacists in the name of anti-racism? Bomb pro-life headquarters in retaliation for bombed clinics? Beat up gay-bashers? People who call themselves our allies are out there doing this shit!

a   And it's illogical. Combating violence with violence means stooping to the same level as those we call fascist. We wipe them out not by beating them into submission, but by engaging in public debate with them, thereby exposing them to the general population as the lunatics they are. Except the cockroaches. The cockroaches we poison.

b   And these debates will convince everyone that we're right and the right is wrong? That their practices are prejudices, that our sins are rights?

a   Not everyone, no, but a lot of people, one at a time. As each

generation becomes more educated, and less influenced by prejudice in their environment, the closer we'll come to a fair and equal society. Have you noticed that ever since the Ku Klux Klan started granting interviews they've become a laughing stock? They still exist and they still do shitty stuff, but they're not the mighty brotherhood they were even ten years ago. They're a bunch of pathetic pencil-dicked morons with fucked-up ideas and pointy-headed clown suits, and anyone with a brain cell knows it. Now shut up and sit on my face.

b   OK, the Ku Klux Klan are laughable, I'll give you that. But there's more than just them. There's others. Young Nazi groups and skinhead white supremacist gangs that kids are joining because they think they're cool and rebellious and radical. And the TV evangelists preaching that gays are indecent, disgusting pedophiles are getting more money and more TV time every day. And there are some states in the U.S. where there are no abortion clinics, not because they're illegal, but because doctors are getting gunned down in front of their houses while their families watch their blood running down their driveways into pools on the street, and racist and homophobic violence is on the rise, and so is domestic violence, and how do we know that all of this isn't an indication that we're fighting a losing battle?

a   It's just like when you spray for roaches and for days afterwards you see more of them than you saw before and in places you never thought you'd see them. It's because they're panicking. Their cockroach instinct is telling them that their time's up and they're running, looking for higher ground. Believe me, it's only a matter of time before they're on their backs, kicking their little legs, screeching, praying up to their Cockroach God, and dying a horrid, agonizing death while we laugh, dance gleefully, and prepare to lay new shelf paper.

b   Kiss me, you fat slut.

a   I understand your question about perception. Of course I understand. But we can't think about that. Should women fighting for the right to vote have stopped to consider that maybe they shouldn't have it? We have to know that our arguments are good and just and moral and fair. Yes, we are being just as intolerant as our opponents. But what they don't tolerate is our love, our pleasure, our choices... What we don't tolerate is bullshit. Get it?

b   But there's still so much old bullshit clogging the pipeline to understanding. Like, how are we supposed to argue that it's not only perfectly normal, but absolutely wonderful for two women to fuck each other, with someone who thinks women shouldn't wear pants?

a   A dying breed, you cheap tart, a dying breed.

b   Hardly. Look around. There's still a huge amount of pressure on women to look feminine, whatever that means. And most homophobia isn't based on religious beliefs ... most of it is just Mr. and Mrs. Joe Suburb freaking out because they can't tell the girls from the boys anymore.

a   Actually, that kind of bugs me too. I want to be able to tell the girls from the boys. And I want to be able to tell the straights from queers. And if that makes me just as much of a bigot as the bigots I hate, then pin me to the couch and fuck me, baby. Fuck me till I'm begging you to stop.

b   Gladly, darling. I appreciate your honesty. Not many queers in your politically-sensitive position would admit so freely to having such a narrow mind. But I suppose we all have our own lines, even where progressive vision is concerned. Again, I mention that perception is a tricky thing.

a   And again, I ask you to stop talking just long enough to drop your pants and squat on my face.

b   But you see, you've exposed yourself now. You draw lines. Not in the same places that moral non-sodomites might draw lines, but you draw them. Pro-choice feminists are good. Anti-porn feminists are ...

a   Frustrated hags who just need a good fuck.

b   Precisely. And you want women to be women, except you want them to be the kind of women that you want them to be, not the kind of women that zealots and Nazis want women to be.

a   Women should be strong and sweet, like the taste of their cunts.
b   I am so turned on by you.
a   Not all feminists are feminist. Not all lesbians are lesbian. Not all anti-racists are anti-racist. Not by my definitions, anyway.
b   Perception, you see?
a   Kiss me.
b   Yes.
a   Kiss me, fondle my breasts, rub your leg against my cunt, and whisper into my ear that you're going to fuck me, fuck me so hard, hard.
b   Yes. Oh, yes.

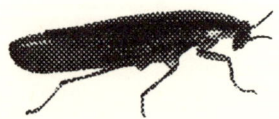

From The True Confessions Of Lana Turner As Told By Her Movies

written by Sky Gilbert

designed by Andy Parks

Corners Lamay
(apologies to that great gay poet: Thornton Wilder)

1. A Typical Day, In Lamay

Don't know what to say, really
Our town's pretty much like any other
I reckon most towns everywhere are the same
People are people, and that's the truth
The name of the town is Corners Lamay
Don't know why it's called that
Can't say
But people have always called it that
And everyone knows better
Than to ask why
As you can see
The lights are beginning to come up
In Corners Lamay
Old Dr. Posh, he's getting out of bed
See him feel his back
That rheumatism is a-hurtin'
He's been pretty busy lately.
There's young Denny Hilts
See, he's openin' up the door of
The Bit and Bite
They're running out of Irish Cream
That Irish Cream is very popular
It's always been that way.
Ron Normand
Picks up his suitcase
Ready to leave for his day job
His cruising clothes are on the chair
He took 'em off in quite a hurry
Last night.
The baths are pretty empty
They've cleaned out all the rooms
Except for the one where Ray Pitumi
Lies sleepin'
Last night he took some Ecstasy
Tricked once or twice
He'll probably sleep 'til noon.

In the park
Josh Pardner
The slow kid they got to help out
He's cleanin' up the used condoms
And the beer bottles
It was a warm night last night
The park was busy
They told him to wear rubber gloves
He does what he's told.
In their black bedroom
Snaz Bizarre
and her girl Giggly
are lyin' abed late
They've got a woman between 'em
A woman who calls herself Mummy
They found Mummy at Rumours, the night before
Mummy opens her eyes
And wonders where she got to
There's a bottle of almost empty poppers
Lying on the floor.

2. Love in Corners Lamay

It's 12 o'clock noon
People have finally rolled out of bed
The Bit and Bite
Is pretty crowded.
Ray Pitumi
Is workin' the room.
He's not wearing a shirt at all really
His blue eyes gleamin'
Anybody want to sit with me?
Share my coffee?
Dr. Posh stops by
He's had a rough morning
Stirs his coffee
Looks around
At who's skinny, sickly
Who he might see next day in his office
Who's takin' care of themselves
Who's not.
Snaz and Giggly
Bought Mummy a donut
They sure don't know how to get rid of her.

Snaz has got a movin' job soon
Doesn't want to leave Mummy with Giggly.
A bit too much chemistry there.
It's a problem.
Josh eyes Ray
Josh might be gay
If only he knew the meaning of the word.
And then Norm rushes in
It's his lunch hour
He just has time to hurry down
And make eyes at young Denny
Doesn't think Denny cares for him
Denny doesn't know how to say it
But he wants a Daddy
"Would you like some extra cream?"
He asks Norm
And at that moment
At the Bit and Bite
At 12:00 noon
When there is no moon
When the sun is near its height
In the early autumn sky
With the babies from Hades
In the prams rushing by
Norm looks at Denny
And Denny looks at Norm
And Norm knows Denny wants a Daddy
And that Daddy might be he.

3. Death in Corners Lamay

Three years have passed
And Denny and Norm have been lovers
For two
Denny doesn't work at the Bit and Bite anymore
Josh is working there
He had his first gay experience
He didn't understand it
But it was lots of fun.
Giggly moved in with Mummy
Snaz got very violent.
But after she threw some furniture 'round
She felt a lot better.
Ray works at the bathhouse now

He tricks between shifts
He organized a drag show for Thursday nights
And Tuesday night pizza
People enjoy that.
At the hospital
Dr. Posh closes
Norm's eyes
Norm just died from Karposi's Sarcoma
Denny is at his side.
Denny closes his own eyes.
"Oh just let me live one day
Just one day over again
Let it be an ordinary day
The most ordinary day
No, let's make it the day
That I told Norm I loved him
Over the Irish Cream
Even tho' I didn't know it"
Yup
Love and death
And an ordinary day
Are the same as anywhere
In Corners Lamay.

Why Sitting Here Watching You Drink Coffee In My Bed Wearing Your Favourite White Bathrobe Of Mine Reminds Me Of My Grandfather (for Shaun)

Well it does
Let me tell you a little bit about my grandfather
He wasn't really my grandfather, I mean
he was my grandmother's second husband and no relation
But he was always the kindest person I ever knew
I mean I knew Mom and Dad didn't really approve
They tried to understand why I rode around town with my
Raggedy Andy doll in my bicycle basket even though the
other boys made fun of me they tried to understand
And my dad tried to play baseball with me and talk
And my mother tried to get me to hold my wrists straighter
But my grandfather who wasn't really my grandfather
he used to take me fishing
and taught me how to use a darkroom
and let me listen to his old classical music
But most of all he had this great old recording of Sweet
Sue, you know "Sweet Sue, that's you!" on an old scratchy
record and usually once every visit he'd pull it out and I'd
put on my special little tap shoes and they'd clear a space
in the den and I'd do my little tap dance to "Sweet Sue" and
my grandmother used to clap and my mother used to laugh
and my father seemed grudgingly, to approve of this
particular peculiarity of mine
And I knew, unbeknownst to them all (or maybe they knew,

hence the suspicions) who I imagined myself to be
I was Shirley Temple
and it was The Littlest Colonel or it was Heidi or it was
Little Miss Marker and whatever scrape I was in, I just knew
I could save the crippled boy and raise the money for the
orphanage if I just did a little tap dancing
You know I think deep down my grandfather, who wasn't
really my grandfather knew that I wished I was thought I
was dreamed I was Shirley Temple and you know I think he
didn't really mind and I don't think he approved or disap-
proved I think he just really loved me and liked it
And so I imagine that today, my grandfather who wasn't
really my grandfather was looking in on us, and he saw us
making lazy love in the morning light and he saw me make
you, a fine strapping young man, a really good cup of coffee, because I like making my man a good cup of coffee,
and then he saw you sitting on my bed reading porno
mags and watching old movies on TV drinking coffee and
wearing your favorite white bathrobe which was mine
And I think he even saw me loving you
And I think he didn't approve or disapprove or anything he
just loved me and really liked it
Do you think that's possible?

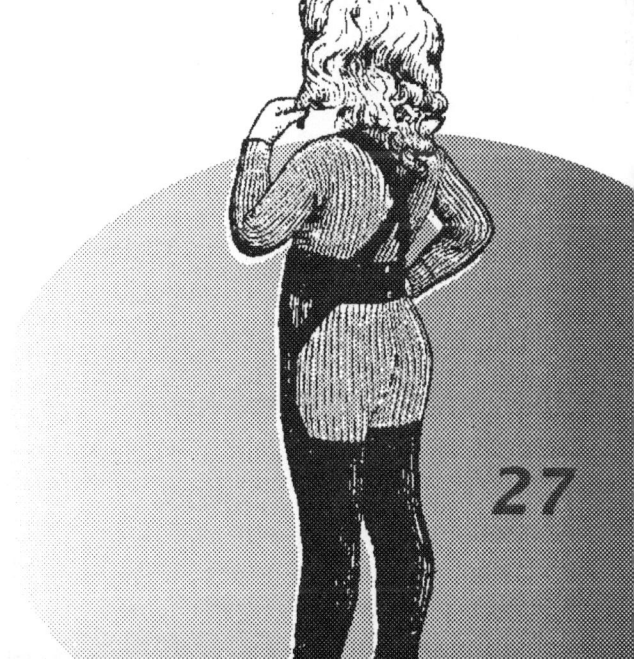

There Will Be No Lizzie Katish

There you stood in front of the mirror
and the snapdragons were dropping their petals
trying on my grandfather's hat
(the horrible grandfather, the fascistic one, the one who
wanted me to fight in the Vietnam War and who wouldn't go
to church unless there was an American flag there and who
didn't speak to me for the last five years of his life well his
loss not mine)
So what am I supposed to tell you, eh?
What do I have to tell you to keep you?
That you are the only one and there will never be anyone
else?
That I'll never want any other boy ever?
That I'll always have your coffee ready on time?
That I'll never ever not want to be with you, unless you don't
want to be with me?
I could say all those things
and that would be the big monogamous lie
but I don't want it to be like that for us
because I still have dreams about my horrible grandfather's
house
and the spiral staircase, and I'm always falling off
And I think of my grandfather dropping dead in the
strawberry patch so what killed him eh?
I think it was the weight of all those lies
Whenever we went driving he used to tell us he was going to
see Lizzie Katish, "Don't tell your grandma", he'd say "I'm
going to see Lizzie Katish" — the other woman and we'd laugh
we'd joke
But I'll bet there really was a Lizzie Katish
There always is a Lizzie Katish
And so what if right now you are my Lizzie, you burn down
the whole town and you're a place to be bad and silly and
irrelevant and dirty and the dark and the balcony and do you
think the people from the press club saw us and you scare me
when I come in the door and say things in the dead of night
that I'm never to repeat ever in the day and I don't (see I
didn't) you're my Lizzie Katish and right now there are no lies
there's nothing to GET AWAY FROM nothing to escape nothing
to hide just the clear moonlight and your pale muscular body
and me I just want to suck on it until you come
So
you stand by the mirror and you gently place the old black
top hat on your head and the snapdragons are losing their
petals and I'm thinking please don't let my horrible
grandfather's hat fit please don't
and it doesn't
and so I'm glad
I can't tell you how glad I am

Confession Number One

Alright, one more
And this is an early movie
One of the earliest The Postman Rings Twice
In Postman Lana is almost quadruply outclassed by the terse, dark script, by the taut direction and by Cecil Kellaway and John Garfield both consummate actors with real talent
But Lana has something that outclasses everything and everyone
The camera loves her in a way that reminds us of what love is all about for just as our eye constantly turns to the loved one to devour to observe every detail every batting of an eye of flinch of muscle the camera cannot get enough of her and she knows it
When she says "I've never been homely but ever since I was fourteen I've never met a man who didn't give me an argument about it"
We understand and we understand that love is an argument and that beauty always wins
Evil again, she pouts and plans but most of all she offers her lips her eyes her hips and those outfits of classic white (a different one in every scene) there is so much to savour
— there's Lana bursting out of the diner in the dead of night in her swimming garb, hair perfectly coiffed and swinging her bathing cap with daring insouciance.
What is more daring even than sex with John Garfield under the moonlight is going swimming with that hairdo
Will it get mussed?
But no, the blindness and faith of moviegoers in the '40s was such that Lana could endure sickness death and even midnight skinny dipping without damaging that hair
And in the silence of his bedroom
For at the crucial moment she slips into John Garfield's bedroom and John Garfield registers for us the ecstasy the surprise the utter delightful confusion of such beauty suddenly appearing in one's bedroom
And Lana quivering there her shoulders hunched intensely as we imagine the fall of her breasts the nipples delicately

grazing the starched white cotton fabric
"A woman needs love."
Yes Lana, yes like John Garfield we forgive your ambition,
we forgive your lies your plotting your planning we even
forgive your fake movie ironing
because we want to kiss you the way we want to kiss that
person we shouldn't, you know the one that every instinct
tells us will lead to sleepless nights and bad phone calls
and a general difficulty in dealing with anything that's
supposed to be important
We want to kiss you the way John Garfield does
And we know that he's whispering to himself
"I must...I must...even if it means my own...someone else's
death...I must kiss her...I must..."
He grabs her shoulders her muscles tense, the lips pout
and they plunge into the darkness, the oblivion, the
ecstasy which is their lust

How Beauty Is Like Eating A Chicken Salad Sandwich

Wake me, I am sleeping
Wake me
Tho' it seems I go about my daily tasks with stunning regularity,
Tho' I seem to know why I exist and exactly where I'm going,
Tho' it seems I work and scrimp and save and blow it all on some holiday,
I'm sleeping
Wake me
I am reminded of an incident at the London Apprentice backroom where I was displaying my tits and my erection and a lad with a shaved head approached produced a huge cock from his striped shorts which I sucked on and then he played with me until I came. "Well," he said, zipping up, hauling it all back in, "at least you woke me up. I was falling asleep."
And that's what it's like isn't it?
You're fast asleep and dreaming.
And all you want is to be woken up to feel touch taste and hear again.
Knowledge is sleep.
Analysis is sleep.
But oh to be awake again to find that in the moment stretched like cellophane over lunch you punch through and there is chicken salad which isn't a preparation for anything else it's not an appetizer it's just dinner and it just is and it's delicious
So,
Tho' I may walk about with wary eye and care,
Tho' I may slowly choose my step and speak only when I dare,
Tho' I may wait and worry, plan and concentrate,
What I want most is,
to be awake
Again
Wake me, beauty,
For I am asleep

Oblong Rhonda Kerouac Meets Dean (Neal) The Viking Holding An Enema Bag

I was thinking about Jack Kerouac
and (his) Dean Moriarty that's
Neal Cassidy and the two of them standing in their t-shirts
like big bosom buddies smiling
And there I was in San Francisco in the selfsame alley
where Jack and Dean (Neal) got drunk and horny and
probably collapsed in a slobbering heap hug 5 a.m. one
cool foggy 1950's night
But they weren't gay (no)
They weren't in LOVE with each other
No, they were just two handsome hairy guys with big
chests and athletic hands and poetic thoughts who were
absolutely obsessed with each other and wrote poems
about each other and went away on long vacations
together and loved and dreamed and even fucked women
in front of each other
But they weren't gay (no)
And I think of Jack hiding that secret from everybody (not
that he really hid it he told everyone about Dean Dean
handsome Dean strong Dean smart Dean sexy Dean but
claimed Dean was only his friend)
Poor alcoholic, religious, Jack like Oblong Rhonda meeting
the Viking
Oblong is plucky but has dark hair and is no match for the
Viking like the poor beat mother she's tired the kid looks at
a picture of Erik the Red — "what's that Momma?" "It's a
Norseman" she says, tired, so tired, "No Momma what is
it?" "IT'S A VIKING!" I want to shout, "TELL THE KID IT'S A
FUCKING VIKING!" and the man with the enema book,
interested in enemas I call a phone number a thin man
opens a tall door at the end of a long hallway "Take this

Beuys

I had my choice between Beuys
and boys
I don't know
Some choose Beuys
Peter did
As for me, though I find Beuys nice
I still choose boys.
After all when Beuys walks into the sea
you know it's because of Kierkegaard or Steiner
But boys
they're a different matter
They walk into the sea because the night calls them
because they're lonely
or because the sea is wet
And they don't ... come back
I repeat, don't
So if I had my choice
I'd take boys
their thighs are bigger
and they don't come back
(sorry, Joseph)

Some Denials
(apologies to Dorothy Parker)

1.
Speaking of your beauty
I've quite had my fill
I mean there won't be any need anymore for me to bring a case of beer and drink it all while getting to know your friends all a pretence for
Kissing you.
One can certainly have one's fill of beauty like yours
For, certainly, to imagine endless draughts of plump buttocks and your youthful flesh hot beneath my hands
Becomes boring after awhile
Ah yes, even as I write this poem, I'm yawning
All I can say is, thank god it's over
Yawn

2.
In another city
I hear a particularly cloying song on the radio; sentimental and romantic, luscious with a sweep of dropping thirds
This music is obviously calculated to make me cry
Of course it's not you I'm crying about
Of course it's my lost youth, and being in a foreign land, and my shoes are too tight and I had to try particularly hard, harder than usual, to get laid last night and I miss my cat
These are quite obviously, pressing concerns which, conspiring with that sudden burst of 11 a.m. San Francisco sun have engineered a predictable response: the fantasy that I miss you.
Knowing this is all the result of a collusion of precipitate coincidental effects I am ultimately unmoved
Yes certainly I am crying, and I conjure up your desperate yet detached 22-year-old kisses warm on my thigh
But these manufactured images soon disappear and I am watching myself cry
And it is all rather comic, really

3.
Having had a lot of men and still thinking of you is the stuff from which a certain kind of melodramatic garbage is made
Certainly either tragedy or farce I shall decide later, which
Ah yes, familiar territory, it's as if the image of you, passionate, bored, the image of you perhaps picking your feet, is so potent, that it travels unalloyed across time and distance pungent, sweat filled, perorated with longing, wet with a certain remembered allegory of some image of youth
of eagerness, of confusion, of conceit which is your personality which I imagine I desire as much as your body

Honestly. You'd think I'd read it all somewhere or made it up.
As if the remembered image of yourself, MR. BEST, in some sort of preoccupied repose could actually bridle my never-ending, ever-changing, obsessive promiscuous desires for
other boys.
Or worse yet, satisfy me?
Even the remembrance of you, sweet enough to satisfy me.
Hah.
It is, after all, a ridiculous concept.

4.
Incongruous with lust and remembrance I, a caped crusader of semi-virile ilk sip cappuccino in a room resplendent with diced queens on coke, bitter they are, and redundant (or did I say that already?) deja vue on the big screen spread eagled bare-breasted (yes you kissed them repeatedly, dare I mistake it for more than duty?) and nonsense seems riddled with the enigma of Russia, wrapped in it, like the revelation that Winnie the Pooh was a bear found in Ontario, brought to England, and that A.A. Milne was not a pederast. Inarticulate with envy for your next lover, I am, yours
truly, denying all, love, me.

5.
I don't want you
I don't need you
I don't regret the flip and perhaps inappropriate postcard I sent you.

When I return home I will have no need to call you.
I certainly have no desire to see you perform in a play
and am not at all interested in whether or not you are
a talented actor.
I have absolutely no intention to lick your bum or to enjoy
you licking mine.
Whether or not you comb your hair or wear short shorts that
barely cover your ass is completely a matter of
indifference to me.
I can't even remember the colour of your eyes
Your hair was brown, wasn't it?
It seems to me you laughed a lot.
Funny, I just can't seem to remember

6.
So this afternoon I will go to a leather-bar tea dance,
and there will be lots of hefty and beefy older men there,
men with experience, tact, men who are good in bed and know
who they are and what they want, which is, more often
than not, me. And I will have a chance to meet someone my own
age, settled, with similar interests and experience,
someone who will see me as a love object instead of the
other way around. What relief. To socialize with men of
a certain age and substance. I'm glad I've grown out of
this obsessive-boy-thing. After all it was only a phase
probably somehow related to a deep inner self-loathing.
But I'm over it now, thank you.

7.
Not your lips
Not your ass
Certainly not the way your talk or laugh or sit carelessly
in a chair
Not your dizzy tendency to forget to call
Not your lack of any real interest in me
No
      None of these things

8.
And I am the Queen of Rumania.

pamphlet" he says "Read it you Viking!" well maybe that's what made Jack Kerouac so profound he was the little Oblong Rhonda with the lonely enema bag and Dean (Neal) was the Viking but he didn't admit it didn't tell anyone so he was brilliant
If you're dishonest and tortured about something it means you'll be a brilliant artist, I guess
And here I am Oblong Rhonda holding the enema bag ("Confess confess it's an old Shaman thing," says Kate whose lanky limbs hide a dick which is now a cunt because she's a lesbian transsexual, Kate who is also a witch beckons me with a skull, she tells ALL including the Shaman's story "You die, the God tells you something, then you come back and the only RULE is you gotta tell everyone the truth or you'll go crazy")
JACK WHY DIDN'T YOU TELL
You wouldn'ta gone crazy if only you woulda told the truth!
Oh I don't know
All I know is I gotta tell it over and over again I'm Oblong Rhonda with the enema bag and you're my Viking young and tall and straight and lean and you make me suck your cock "This is the last time I'll be ordering you around for awhile" you say and you won't hold my hand in public and you're very strange about kissing
I gotta tell gotta tell it all
or else I'll go mad
Poor mad Jack like Oblong Rhonda crazy with the kissing lying kissing lying kissing lying

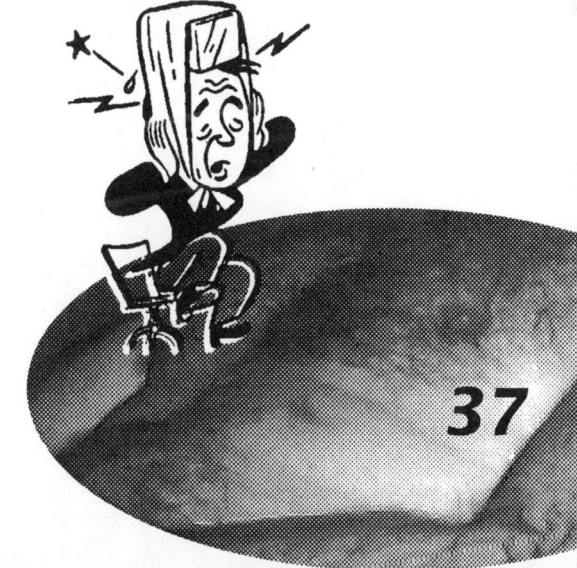

Eight Poems Of Advice From A French Whore To A Young, Handsome Flirtatious Cowboy Embarking On A Career In Literature

1.
Merci beaucoup je suis tu es il est elle est nous sommes
vous etes ils sont elles sont avez-vous une plume de ma
tant amour buckets oui oui ou no ou maybe

2.
Can't think of what to say really
'cause you've got a car and a coyote
and a dream
But someone like you shouldn't be let loose on the world
without a little advice
So here's some:
drive careful boy
but not too careful
and when you get stoned
write things
'cause it's on those lonely nights on the road
I mean range
when those cowboys really let loose
And then there's the bunkhouse
And what's really between your legs, huh?
Is it a dick?
Sorry I got out of control
But just remember
when you sit on couches with venerable playwrights like me

don't touch them cowboy
unless you want to get touched back

3.
Be ambitious
but only for your work because
only work matters
Don't look at me like that with your big brown eyes or are they
blue
just don't
Ambition is this thing that will kill you if it's money fame and
power
But what doesn't kill you everything does
But no listen don't laugh
you've got this thing this need
so do it want it
but want to create a world that's not real life because
what else is there to want
but what there isn't?
And when they tell you that you have to learn about the here
and now and your fellow man and write about what you know
then get in your old Mustang put the dog in the front seat
have a few tokes and drive off into the prairies with your very
own space aliens from Mars

4.
Be promiscuous
but only with your body
The body
sorry — bullshit your body
was made to be touched
especially your buttocks
(you wouldn't want to be touched there would you?)
Well sorry that's what bodies
are for
But your mind
your feelings
your emotions
they are for those special people who understand
they are for me
And if I seem aloof or distant or thoughtful or drunk
I probably am
But I'm probably wondering what it would be like if I had
everything if everything was mine if and I can imagine it late
at night we've driven off somewhere it's a country road flat the

land is flat but not you you have all these curves and
humps and hardnesses just proof that a cowboy is not the
prairies he's the opposite he goes up and down
and I'm caressing your incredibly thick legs
and the dog is in the backseat
with an erection
and the moon is full
The dog barks he wants you too
but he can't have you
We wrestle, the dog and me over you
I'm dead ripped apart
he's chewing on my bones
and later there will be vultures
but I will have had you, cowboy

5.
Don't say you didn't flirt
I don't care if you didn't flirt
Don't say you didn't flirt
because you flirted okay?
Saying you didn't flirt is the first
sign of flirting okay?

6.
Do not hurt ladies
Don't lie to them
Don't turn up without calling
And by ladies I mean anyone who wears a dress
because you seem to go for that kind
the ones with makeup and hair and nails and helplessness
ladies like me
But don't hurt us
We don't mind being devoured by dogs over you no
but we don't like being left crying in cars
our dresses hiked up over our heads
We're pretty and we want to stay that way
And we're not cowgirls
we're different from you
we wear high heels and perfume and smell like Paris
just because of some mother who didn't treat you right
and doesn't understand you
don't give everything in a dress a hard time
We like you hard
us ladies with our foreign accents
but only down there

40

7.
Mon petit...Milord...ne venez pas...restez ici...s'il vous plait...je vous aime...je suis...empty...sans vous...Hallo...charmant...big one...Ne venez pas Non Non!

8.
And finally
Don't take advice
from elderly playwrights like me
who dream they are French whores
The ones who look at you sadly at parties
and want to see you bare-assed, wearing nothing but your cowboy hat
Don't take advice from us
'cause we're whores after all
and there will be other cowboys
But this whore will always remember the one
who liked to drive away and never come back
and who laughed like my first best friend
and who touched me too much for a straight guy
and who wore pants that were too tight
and who had a very strange relationship with his dog
This whore is thinking about you now
and that means you are here
I close my eyes
there you are

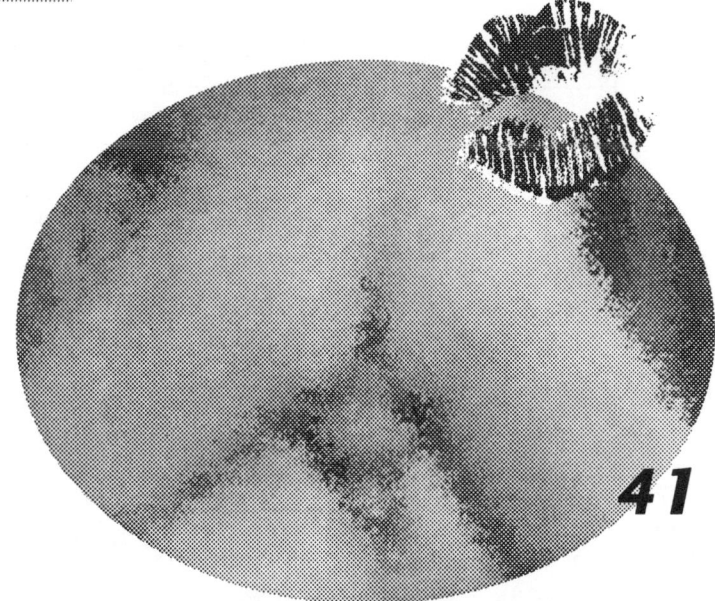

MASS IN B FLAT
in memory of a young man's poetry floating (burning) away

prologue:

We call on Harvath, Grog, Enwhistle, Hundertwasser, the great gods of the Vikes to bless this bastion this traveller this floating emissary to the world beyond Gundrag, Hipbath, Hondle, Hooper, Logo, Arat, Gods of heaven sea and ships to guide this deadly mass upon its way.

introit:

what is it	what?
what is in this	in this?
in this bundle	this bundle?
this bundle of	bundle of
papers	paper
that we are burning	are burning
they belong to	belong to
a young lad	a mere lad
I said young lad	young lad
of twenty	twenty
how young	young

gradual:

Bless the lord for he maketh young men twenty years old
RESPONSE — For his mercy endureth forever
For he maketh them young, he maketh them randy, he maketh them homosexual
RESPONSE — For his mercy endureth forever
For he maketh them lie in my bed and make strange noises and giggle and hide their faces in the pillow and read poetry and kiss and deny kiss and deny
RESPONSE — For his mercy endureth forever
Bless the lord for giving them brains as well as loins those 20-year-olds, but most of all for allowing them to stay twenty for one whole year.

RESPONSE — For his mercy endureth forever
Bless the lord for giving them the intelligence to laugh at
my jokes, the irony to see that I'm not always funny, the
vulnerability to apologize for being late, the lack of experience to allow me to appear wise
RESPONSE — For his mercy endureth forever
But most of all thank the lord for girding their loins, fur-
ring their thighs and strengthening their buttocks even
though no sign of earthly battle is imminent
RESPONSE — For his mercy endureth forever

tract:

A young man is nice
when he likes you
He's better it's true
when he loves you
But these things
(it must be said)
are usually decided in bed!
And bed
is a strange place
to think

dies irae:

Dies irae die ila solvet saeclum in favilla TESTES DAVID
CUM (shyly) sibilla

sanctus

What we have here is a pile of a glorious pile of papers
What is — what is in them you may ask?
The writings of a young man of barely twenty!
Ah!
What beauty what inarticulate inchoate testicular variety?
What divine anarchism, plunging masochism, plentiful
engorged playthings of the mind?
He wants to destroy these things because he has grown
out of them
Ah hah, we say, we know
Who knows?
For they were written before England, before Europe,
before Ceylon
Ah hah!

Alack and alas
When he was a teen?
Are we eager?
Do we preen to see what is about to be burned?
But no, like the pile of books in the woodshed, like the
teddy bear under the sofa, like the wad of Kleenex beside
the bed, what is being burned shall never be seen by men
God, or (heaven forbid) his mother

agnus dei:

Buried deep
Buried deep
Buried deep within him
Buried deep
Buried deep are secrets we shall never know
Secrets we shall never know
Adolescent secrets
floating on Lake Ontario
sailing off to Buffalo?
Secrets!
Secrets we shall never know
Search him high and
search him low
Secrets buried deep
within him!
Secrets we shall never know
(pause)
Take off your shorts

benedicamus domino:

Let us bless the lord for he certainly knew what he done in
making you
You couldn't have been a mistake, though my eyes might
be a mistake and my thoughts about you
We never flew, 'tis true, like these papers which are
disappearing somewhere into Northern Ontario
But still I discern somewhere nay further than that away,
over the mountain hidden somewhere in the way you smile
and say "Yes" there is a shall we say...profundity?
Dare we? True love, like death answers yes when you least
expect it
You have all the attractiveness of a gun half-cocked and
your oneness baffles me, makes me humble, effective,

weak in the knees
Let us bless the lord for if he made a mistake in you, he made a good one and he followed it consistently to its mistaken end, giving you long eyelashes and this poetry to send out to sea
If a fish finds it he may smell your eyes in the ashes, feel your laugh, breathe in the odour of your generosity
Being a teenager is gone now!
Grow up
Take hold
The comedy turns to tragedy which when viewed through long eyelashes looks like a particularly juicy episode of Dynasty
Farewell teen years
It's your party
You can cry, if you want to

epilogue

Heth, Grent, Bumble, Ackerwathe, lords of fish and lords of sea, bless this vessel, which though weak might make it to Toronto Island
Remember that you can't kiss an 18-year-old in broad daylight unless he's a different sex than you, and that makes life tough
Grunt, Saxe, Indlebung, Grath, Og, Mog, Gorgor take your money, take your youth, take these poems, and run

The Sign At Massimo's

At Massimo's there is a sign and it has a picture of two pizzas:
"ours",
and "theirs"
Now "our" pizza is really plump and hot and juicy and done in nice colours
But "their" pizza is kind of yellow and dry and cold looking and it's not as big as "ours"
and it's sitting in a much duller looking room
There is a lesson in the Massimo's pizza sign
and I try to apply it to my life
That is, I sincerely wish that I could — that there was a sign that said OUR life and THEIR life and all you had to do was pick the more attractive life with the good colouring and the bright room
I mean but who would pick the dry, little life with the bad colours?
Not me
Just stupid people
At Massimo's, Massimo with the cigarette the hair the smooth moves, he stands on the corner and he is eternally twenty, Massimo lifts a finger and nods and we know...
"This way to the right life."

Closure

written by Timothy Archer • designed by Mike O'Connor

48 — Closure

As children, Claire and Tom played the game of blindfolds. They'd made it up themselves. The game had no goal; nothing was sought to be won; blindfolds gave them an opportunity to role play.

They played the game, like most others — Monopoly, checkers, Risk — in the basement of Tom's parents' bungalow. Claire's mother usually deposited her here in order to run errands. The two children retreated to the rec room, with juice and a plate of cookies, ostensibly to get out from under Tom's mother's feet. But there were better reasons. Sometimes his mother left them alone for an hour or so. She never told Claire's mother this and made them promise to keep quiet. They wouldn't tell a soul.

As soon as the front door closed, they hurried to his mother's sewing corner. A bin stood beside the work table. It contained fabric scraps.

First Tom tied a piece around Claire's eyes. Then, still blindfolded, she did the same for him. Claire operated well without sight.

The play opened with each of them facing the other, an arm's length apart. "Ready?" she would ask. "Ready," he'd reply.

A moment of silence let them submerge their personalities. One would reach out to touch the other, their breathing quick with anticipation. The air smelled of apples and shortbread. Contact allowed them to speak and whoever spoke first led. Sometimes neither coveted the position.

Once, Claire took hold of Tom's wrist and said: "Doctor, my vulva hurts." She proceeded to guide his hand to where and pressure it to how much. Another time Tom rested both hands on her chest, ran them down to her groin, and when the silence still ensued, said: "Mister Prime Minister, we have to find out why your penis is missing."

On those afternoons they never cast off their clothes entirely. Tom's mother returned sometime and they had to be cautious. Only when they heard the front door open did they drop the blindfolds and see each other's nudity. Invariably they'd giggle.

The game ended forever when they were eleven. It was fall. Dead leaves were burning somewhere down the lane. Claire's hair hung so straight; her mother might have ironed it. Her blindfold that day was a paisley print that had lined a jacket. Tom's mother had a prescription to fill. They had eaten a plate of peanut butter

cookies. His blindfold came from curtain fabric: ivory, with gold pinstripes. The front door closed. Claire began.

Hands on his shoulders. "Lay down."

He did. His head touched the empty plate. He pushed it away.

Hand on his knees, pushing, spreading; Claire lay on top of him. "Put your knees up and cross your ankles over me."

He did. He let his heels sink into her corduroy skirt.

Claire breathed peanut butter into his face. "You bitch," she said. She sounded close to tears. Her pelvic bones ground against his own. They sucked in each other's air.

"Who are you?" he asked.

"I'll tell you when I'm good and ready."

He slipped a hand between their bodies, pushed into her skirt, under her panties. His fingers found the groove of her sex, and unexpected moisture. He pulled his hand free. He wanted to look at his fingers, to see them glisten in the half-light of the basement, but he didn't dare remove the blindfold. Instead he pressed his finger to her lips, then down her chin. "I know who you are," he said.

"Shh." Quietly. Then, in even more of a whisper, "Shut up."

He took her hand and put it between them on his erect penis. "You're Claire," he said. "You're Claire and I'm Tom."

She wrenched herself away and off of him. He heard the air rushing towards him before he felt the stinging slap. He saw a flash of white. He could hear Claire breathing heavily. He pulled the blindfold down his face. Claire already had hers around her neck. A fingerprint of blood marred her lips and chin.

"Never do that again," she almost shouted. "Never call me that again."

❧

Christmastime is social time. Friends I've seen only twice during the year call up to demand a get-together. It's an excuse to drink, so why not? Forget that shopping; forget that half-finished book; forget that soiled laundry. Get drunk. Get festive.

And this Christmas was no different, only more so. I wouldn't be flying

home to see my parents. I'd spent a good portion of my savings on a debauched holiday out west. It had left me with little other than sunny photographs, tan lines and a half-used bottle of Kwellada. And my parents, living the financially cautious lives of retirees, couldn't spring for the ticket, even as a gift.

This extended my Yuletide revelries.

And so this Christmas I was walking home from one of these parties. Home from Kensington Market to my ghetto apartment. It felt good to be out in the cold air after all the body heat and cigarette smoke in the people-cramped house.

Cocaine-wasted David had hosted the party, filling the place with the usual assortment of affected wannabees and ghosts of friendships past. I held the latter post. The last time I'd seen David had been at the opening for his new show, back in August. Both times I noted the grasping look in his eyes, as though he wanted to say, 'Get me out of here, Tom. This isn't my scene anymore. Take me somewhere calm. Take me somewhere new.' Either that or he wanted to sleep with me again. I couldn't help because David can't change. He'd continue on this track until his septum fell or his T-cell count precluded such activity.

David's a friend I can love and avoid. It felt good to leave the house. The city's silence surprised me after the glut of music and babble. On a weeknight, two days before Christmas, I expected a little more traffic. But even on Bay Street the cars travelled infrequently.

And after a slow walk north, even that became annoying; I craved a greater silence. I headed down Grosvenor, towards the Y. It seemed quiet enough here.

The huge empty block, where my favourite Indian restaurant once stood, had been dusted with snow earlier in the evening. It wouldn't last. As soon as the sun hit, it'd turn to slush like everything else this winter. I lit a cigarette and continued walking. Looking behind me I could see my footprints on the sidewalk. They'd be gone soon too.

"Hey, bud, you got a light?"

I hadn't seen the guy standing by the alley. He was young, maybe 17. He wore torn jeans and shivered slightly inside a couple layers of denim.

A zit hid under his jaw.

"Yeah, sure." I shielded the flame from the wind. With the cigarette burning, he tilted his head up, clicked his jaw and exhaled. "Thanks, man."

"Never a problem." I smiled. He returned a conspiratorial grin. I thought I could pick him up, but I also knew he was working. I walked away.

Headlights illuminated my feet. Whoever drove the car was probably looking for something to rent that night. I stopped and turned to see what he looked like, to stare him down.

I was both relieved and disappointed by the plainness of the car: a Taurus. It crawled slightly past me, then stopped. I could see the man's silhouette but no features. He turned to look at me and waited. He raised a hand, and in a quick motion, beckoned.

What the hell, I thought, I've met whores before, I may as well meet one of their dates. It would be an experience. I walked slowly towards the driver's window. The man inside reached over and unlocked the passenger door.

Just like that? He wanted me to get in just like that? I stopped by the driver's side and gave the man a slanted grin.

His 50 years hung from his face lightly, and his thin hair revealed a pink scalp that the street lights only made pinker. His gaze darted from side to side and into the rear-view mirror. He seemed too nervous to be a cop. Even if he sped off with me riding shotgun, I could always tumble out at the first stoplight.

I walked around the Taurus and opened the passenger door. "Hi," I said, leaning down.

"Hello," he replied, a trace of gravelly phlegm in his throat. "Want to talk?"

"Sure." I got in and settled beside him. I shut the door. At the very least I'd have an interesting story to tell friends tomorrow.

"Nice night out," he said.

"Sure, very Christmassy."

"Ah, you going anywhere?"

"No, not really." I didn't know how this guy would get to his point. I wasn't about to guide him. But since I'd been standing in the street, since I'd come over when he beckoned, since I'd climbed into his car, I decided to

keep up the momentum. "I was just looking for something to do before I headed home."

"Ah, yeah, well, would you like to go to a party?"

"I just came from one."

He laughed. "Are you up for another one? With me?"

"That depends," I said. "Who's going to be there?"

"Oh, ah, you, of course. And me."

"No one else?"

"No one else."

"Hmm. Well, I don't know. What kind of party would this be?"

"Um, ah, well, you and me." He stared at the dash lights and ran his fingers quickly back and forth on the steering wheel. "I want to blow you and I want you to blow me."

For a moment I thought of the money, but another concern overrode that: could I get it up for this man?

I thought of the money again. Whatever he gave me would probably fund a comforting Christmas dinner at Joso's; and since I wouldn't have my family's cuisine to placate me, I should treat myself. Besides which, I have an imagination, and that alone can make me hard. "Sounds okay." I had to be coy. I still worried that he might be a cop. "But parties can run up a bill."

"Depends," he said. "Depends on the party. Ah. Well, how much do you think this sort of party would cost?"

I didn't want to name a price. I didn't even know the going rate. I squirmed the words out. "Parties ... parties cost more depending on where they take place. For instance, here in this car, is less than someplace roomier."

"I don't want a blow job in my car," he said with disdain. The force of the response startled me. It also made me think that this man was about as experienced at this as I was, maybe only a little more so. If he was a cop, he was a great actor.

I dropped the coyness. "It's your call, mister."

"My name's Bill."

"Bill. Alright, Bill, I can take care of what you want, but you have to let me know if it's worthwhile."

He looked at me and looked away, out at the lobby of the Y. He looked at

the dash lights like they might be a clue. "Forty," he said, a sullen note wrapped around trepidation.

"Forty in the car," I replied. I thought, I'm bartering. I thought, I have a head for business. I thought, I can whore.

"And if we go back to my place?"

"Sixty."

He drummed his fingers on the wheel. He clicked his teeth. Had I outpriced myself? He pushed the standard shift into gear. "Done," he said.

※

We entered a narrow townhouse and he flicked on the entrance light. From where we stood I could see into the living room. He'd made a brave attempt at disguising the modernity of the place: painted the walls deep red, hung heavy curtains with tasselled sashes, furnished the place with faux Queen Anne chairs and a heavy Victorian couch, potted plants in carved boxes. A fake granite obelisk stood in one corner. I recognized it from a time when Claire had sold them from her now-defunct interior design store. It fit a mental image I had of brothel sitting rooms. Very apt for my little foray.

"Ah, you can take off your jacket," he said. He dropped his keys on a shelf by the coat rack. "Would you like, um, something to drink?" His back was to me as he walked into the room.

"Sure. You got scotch?"

"Scotch? Yes. Yes, scotch." He looked over his shoulder at me. "Come in. No need to stand at the door all night. At least I hope not." He gave a nervous schoolboy laugh.

"Shoes?" I called. I heard him opening cupboards in an unseen room.

"You can wear them."

I walked though the living room and into the kitchen. I suppose the juxtaposition of the two rooms wasn't such a shock to me because everything in the living room had been manufactured in this century.

All the surfaces here shone white, lacquered and glimmering. Even the sink was porcelain, rather than the expected chrome. Bill had two tumblers on the counter, and the fridge open getting ice. When I entered the room he

said nothing but smiled and winked. I detected a faint tremor in his hand when he put the ice in the glasses.

At that point in the evening I knew how to wield power. I was desirable. Enough so that someone wanted to pay me for my sex. Never had I felt that surge of confidence with any of the men I'd dated. I'd always gone after the ones that made me hard and weak and swollen with lust. My power over them never entered into it. But here and now, just the thought of a good price tag on my dick made it fill with blood.

"Chivas or Glen Livet?" he asked.

"Livet. I lives for me Livet."

He gave that nervous laugh again. I watched him carefully as he opened another cupboard and took the Glen Livet down, still in its box. Here was a man I didn't desire in the least, whose history I could care less about, and whose affected manner of dress and furnishing I found facile and wanting; and yet I would allow him access to my body. Curious. I almost laughed.

"Amusing thought?" he asked. He handed me the scotch. I leaned in and kissed him, greedily taking his lips within my own. He opened his mouth and I licked his teeth.

Bill pulled away. "You're a fast one, aren't you? I want this to happen upstairs." He led the way. The ice sounded in our glasses all the way up to the second floor. He left the hallway dark. In a room near the front of the house he turned on a standing lamp.

This room was more comfortable; this room was relaxed. An entertainment unit filled one wall, with a 24 inch TV, VCR, laser disc and CD player, tape deck, two turntables and rows and rows of discs, tapes and vinyl. A wide, lumpen sofa faced this. Deep scratches marked the padding of one arm, but I had yet to find other any evidence of a cat here.

In this room Bill's manner changed. He set his drink down on an end table. He wasn't smiling or laughing anymore. "Here," he motioned to the far wall. "Stand over there. You don't need your drink. Here." He took it from me, placed it on the shelves beside a Bill Evans boxed collection.

I stood against the wall facing him. He had his hands in his pockets, shoulders tensed, staring at me as though forming a challenge into words. I leaned back. I let my shoulders rest on the wall, cocked my hip and folded my arms.

"So, how's it going to be?" I asked; huskily, I hoped.

"I'd like — " He coughed. "Just a second." He coughed some more. "Hold on." He went to the shelves and pulled down a Polaroid camera. "I'd like a picture of you."

I thought about it. I didn't want to turn up in the homegrown porn pages of some meat mag. But I had nothing to lose by it either. "Pictures are extra," I answered.

"Not of you naked. Just your face."

I paused. "Pictures are extra."

Bill looked down at the camera. "How much extra?"

"Thirty." It's great to be wanted.

"Thirty? Christ. Fifteen."

"Twenty-five."

"Twenty."

"Twenty-five."

"Twenty-five, and you leave your underwear here when you go."

I considered. I was wearing an old pair of Stanfields. My mother had given them to me as a stocking stuffer three years ago. "Sure."

He came in close with the camera.

"Do you want me to smile?"

"Yeah. You have the nicest smile."

I gave him that grin he liked so much. Then I thought of him beating off to this picture tomorrow night and my smile grew.

"Very nice. Very nice." The flash went. The motor wound. The light left an after image on my retina, but I dimly saw Bill snatch at the Polaroid. He set the camera on the shelf beside a thick pile of pictures. He waved the square slowly in the air trying to speed the chemicals. "Coming," he muttered. "It's coming. Coming. Very nice. Yes. Very nice." He looked back up at me as though he'd forgotten I was in the room.

"What now?" I asked.

He put the Polaroid on the pile by the camera. "Take off your clothes." He stuffed his hands back in his pockets.

I unbuttoned my shirt slowly. I pulled out the front and tail but left it on, hanging open. "Nice chest," he said. Even if Bill gave the commands, he knew the power dynamics here, and I think he resented it. He remained stock still, but the way his knees bent I knew he was restless.

I shrugged the yoke of the shirt and let it drape from my elbows. I unbuckled my pants. My feelings in the kitchen had been an indication, but still I was surprised how my desire responded to this play. An exhibitionist, and I never knew it. I unzipped. I readjusted the bulge in my Stanfields so the head of my cock peeked over the top of the waistband.

From the direction of his eyes, I could tell my winning smile didn't interest Bill so much anymore. He shifted his hands in his pockets. One hand came up and rubbed his forehead. I kicked off my shoes: toe to heel, toe to heel. I let the weight of the belt carry my pants down. I stepped out of them. I let my shirt fall off my wrists. I eased the waistband of the underwear down my stiff cock until it rested under my balls, and I let it snuggle up tight.

Bill rushed forward, tearing his hands from his pockets. His full body hit me. My head struck the wall. For a moment I recalled the Polaroid flash. And after the numb shock of it all I felt his lips and hands. He kissed my neck, my jaw. He bit my lip. One hand gripped my testes, tight and possessive. The other clawed at my chest. Fingers found my nipple and he twisted. Pain and gooseflesh rippled towards my shoulder. I sucked air between my teeth. "You like that, don't you, whore," he muttered.

"Yeah, give me more," I whispered. He was paying me. For a moment I had been stunned and frightened. But this groping reassured me. It was like a four-year-old being presented with a puppy. How could he not maul this gift?

But he stopped. He stepped back. He rubbed his forehead again. "I've got to go to the bathroom for some stuff." He seemed a bit dazed and preoccupied. He turned, walked, stopped. Turned back. "Lie down on the couch." To the door. Stop. Turn. "Play with yourself." Gone.

Jerk off? Why not? I did as he instructed. The sofa was as comfortable as it looked. I pulled off my underwear and shot it towards my other clothes. I took my cock in hand. But I wanted a scotch.

I stood and retrieved it from the shelf. Drank. It felt like burning syrup

down my throat. I went back to the couch. Lying there, I wondered how long this would be interesting. Already, with Bill gone, I felt not-exactly-turgid. Maybe he'd be flattered by the thought. But I continued with his instructions and found myself languidly enjoying the moment. No rush. It even bored me a bit. I wondered if there was a CD I could put on. Something cool; something very alto saxophone.

I stood again; gulped the Livet. I started liking Bill by looking at his collection. He owned discs by Bill Evans, Coleman Hawkins and Randy Weston; Blossom Dearie, Billy Eckstine and Sarah Vaughan. But he'd bought a good variety of other artists as well: The Kronos Quartet, David Danovich, Ute Lemper, and everything I'd ever seen by John Corigliano and John Adams. I thought it strange that the other rooms didn't reflect his personality as this one did. He hadn't even projected a morsel of this self in the car on the way here.

I've always looked at the music in strangers' houses. Music is emotion. And people usually pursue music privately. Any collection will reflect the personality of the owner. I had trouble connecting Bill with his CDs. He seemed too tight, too closed. But he'd brought me here, hadn't he? Into this room. And he'd taken my picture. At once I felt guilty about my humour over his masturbating to my image. Shouldn't I have been flattered as at all other times?

My erection had flagged considerably. And now all I wanted to do was please this man. But it seemed impossible looking at these discs. I knew I couldn't be turned on by a man who hid himself like this, who erected a barrier before such emotion. I wanted natural men. This one was too stunted. Leave him to the professional prostitutes: they could fuck and not care about it. Me? I had thought making a bit of extra money might be nice. I just hadn't thought of the consequences.

But I was here now. I was in this room now. Bill released his passion here. I chose *Bill Evans Live in Paris 1972*, slipped it in the player and switched on the whole mechanism. I lay back on the couch and got back to work. I didn't think of Bill. Either one.

The only thing on my mind was the insistent fact of sensation on my flesh. That was enough for now.

And then it wasn't. How much time had passed? Ten minutes? Count them and it's a long time. Too long for someone to get 'some stuff' from the bathroom.

"Hey, Bill," I called. "Come and share the moment."

No answer. Not even a sound from down the hall. I waited. "Bill?"

Nothing. I got up. The sound of applause came from the speakers. I went to the door and looked down the hall. A sliver of light illuminated the baseboards further down. "Bill?" I walked to the bathroom door. I couldn't even hear water running. I leaned my ear against the door. Quiet. I knocked. "Need a hand? Bill?" I tried the doorknob. Unlocked. I pushed it open.

Bill sat on the toilet, pants around his ankles. He'd slid forward on the seat. His arms hung slack. He had an expression on his face like someone had just set off a firecracker behind him. The scarlet of broken veins completely coloured the white of one eye.

"Jesus Christ!" I rushed in and grabbed his shoulders. He slumped. "Bill, Jesus, Bill." I shook him. His head lolled. "Wake up. Snap out of it. Wake up." My shouts and shaking had no effect. I pressed my ear to his chest. In his body I heard a silence as loud as the bathroom had been moments before. "Oh fuck, Bill. Fuck, fuck, fuck." I pushed him back, pulled his head backwards. I forced his chin down with the palm of my hand. His tongue lay in his mouth like something unrecognizable and exotic at a deli counter. I pinched his nostrils. This man may live, I told myself. You are not about to put your mouth on a corpse's.

I took a deep breath, leaned down, sealed our mouths and blew. Turned my head. Listened. Turned back. Blew. Listened. Blew. Listened.

I don't know how many times I did this, but eventually I knew it was for nothing. The man was as dead as they get. I leaned against the vanity. "Some load of fun you got me into, Bill." I thought maybe I should call the paramedics. Maybe. What good would they do? This man needed a toe-tag.

And I realized I was naked; naked in a bathroom with a corpse who had his pants around his ankles. Quick, I thought, someone take a picture; it's a Kodak moment.

I rushed down the hall. A chill touched my back. Clothes. I needed my clothes. In the entertainment room Bill Evans swung achingly on *A Waltz for*

Debbie. I pulled on the underwear, then pants. I gathered my shirt.

And a sense of deja vu struck me. You've been here before, an interior voice told me. I knew I hadn't, but my movements just then, the crumpled shirt in my hand, the shadows in the corners, all suggested it to me. You've been here before. I could sense it like an aura but couldn't see the connection. You're here again.

No. I pushed the thought away. I put on the shirt and fumbled nervously with the buttons. Halfway up, I remembered the Polaroid. Shit. I was here and they would know it. I felt convinced of some conviction in the near future. I shook so badly that when I grabbed for the Polaroid, the entire pile spilled onto the floor. A sob rose in my throat. I choked on it and that sounded like a laugh. Then I did laugh. Terribly. Sickeningly. To stop it I held my breath. The moment passed.

On the floor before me lay a multitude of white-framed faces. Young men, middle-aged men, women at various stages of aged grace, stared up at me. Some smiled. A few had been photographed in this room. Others had been captured in offices, restaurants, street corners and building entrances. Where was I?

My eye caught on a piece of blue, the colour of these walls. Another boy. My eyes searched but came back to the picture. It was me; me with that fucking full-of-myself grin. I reached for it but stopped.

A few inches away a picture of my childhood friend Claire peeked from underneath two men. I hadn't spoken to her in a couple of years and this seemed to be the period from when the picture was taken. She had her hair in a bob, hennaed to a colour more fierce than her natural brown. Her smile was indulging; not the least forthcoming. Get it over with, she seemed to be telling the photographer, I'm busy. Typical Claire.

I picked it up. Bill had written a date at the bottom of it from just few months before we had last spoken.

So, this trick, just-dead Bill, had known my Claire. I stopped shaking. My breathing steadied. The connection between the two of them acted as a salve on my nerves, but I didn't know why. I embraced that unexpected calm. It seemed better than heart palpitations.

I thought of calling Claire right then. It may have been one in the morning, but people expect news of death and calamity when the phone rings at this hour. Still, it had been two years; our last conversation had been particularly unpleasant, ending with the words 'cocksucker' and 'cunt'. I decided not to call.

I picked up my own picture, joined it with Claire's, and put the two in my front pocket. I finished buttoning my shirt. I tucked it in. All those strangers' faces on the floor seemed to be watching these actions and it gave me the creeps. I needed my peace and wouldn't allow an intrusion. I gathered them up and set the pile where they'd been before.

I left the room, left the light on, left the stereo playing, left the bathroom door open, left Bill alone. I wouldn't touch anything else, I decided. I'd walk to the subway and call the ambulance from there. I just wanted out of the house.

Three steps down the stairs, a curiosity overtook me. Why would a man take so many Polaroids of people's faces? These weren't casual party-time pictures. They were more like records — passport photos or mug shots. It was as though Bill had been conducting a study. But of what? Claire had been part of it. I had been part of it. The others probably knew as much about this as I did. The only person who could tell us the purpose was dead, 20 feet from where I stood.

Someone should know, I decided. This shouldn't be silenced by an executor or beneficiary.

I walked back up the stairs and into the entertainment room. The ice in my scotch had melted. I took the pile of Polaroids down and sat on the sofa. Methodically I flipped each picture off the top, examined it and put it at the bottom of the pile. Faces. Only faces. They held nothing in common but the photographer. A few I vaguely recognized: the owner of an antique market, a waiter, a bar-boy, a vagrant.

A vagrant? I held this one closer. Definitely: the Recipe Man. I used to see him on my way to work for at least two years. Usually he'd sit in a doorway, grizzled, dirty, covered in a blanket with his palm held out. He'd mumble, "Quarter please. Quarter please," to passersby. But some days he'd be up and moving. And he didn't just walk, he lumbered recklessly. These times he'd bellow at people, "First of all you need a bag, a whole bag

of potatoes and you boil 'em to shit. For good measure you'll need a quart of butter, but that's just to make the mix fuckin' nice. Salt's good and so's pepper, but never forget the goddamn milk." Sometimes he'd tell you how to make a caesar salad or chicken kiev. It might have been funny, but the Recipe Man looked frightened when he did this. With eyes wide and darting and the cords on his neck standing out. He seemed aware of what he was doing, but unable to stop himself. He looked horrified by his lack of self-control.

Bill had deemed it necessary to take his picture. The only people I knew who photographed the homeless were bleeding-heart artists and publicists for halfway homes. Bill was obviously neither.

I had to assume that the photography wasn't a whim. The dates on the pictures stretched back six years. The people had to mean something to him. A record of an event? That would be true in my case. Maybe some of them were constant contacts, people he dealt with in daily life. But why would he need a reminder? Especially of the Recipe Man.

I finished the pile. It left me with a clue, but no answers. I put it back. The scotch looked inviting so I took a sip.

This room with its sparse furnishings and open shelves could hide nothing. To get my answers I'd have to search somewhere else. I'd have to be thorough. I'd start with the bedroom.

But first a change of music. I needed a voice to keep me company, so I stopped the Bill Evans. I scanned the collection. Jimmy Scott's most recent would do nicely. I laid it in the tray and pressed play. A muted trumpet drifted through the speakers, then the voice, so worn and melancholy.

I walked down the hallway slowly. I had to pass the bathroom. I knew that, but why hadn't I thought of it before? My mouth dried up. I peered around the door-jamb. Bill looked pasty under the fluorescent lights. He was so inert he seemed more waxwork than human.

Jimmy Scott sang in the other room, with a high-pitched and grandmotherly voice. I reached in and shut the door on Bill. I didn't need to look at him. I knew he was there. I didn't want to be reminded.

I hurried to the bedroom and turned on the lights. Bill definitely was not a pack rat. There was a bed, a dresser, a side table and a lamp. No clutter. The furniture had been made in another era, all painstakingly tooled walnut pieces.

Maybe he kept the surfaces clean to avoid marking them. A silver framed picture stood on the dresser: a portrait from the '30s of a young couple, stern and concentratedly staring. Probably his parents. I picked it up. Nothing had been written anywhere and it had a felt base. It left no marks.

I opened the dresser drawers to find undershirts, socks, boxer shorts, sweaters, turtlenecks, knit t-shirts. Nothing had been hidden underneath.

But the bottom drawer contained dirty laundry: three pairs of bikini briefs, two jockstraps and an undershirt with faint, stiff stains. Lining the drawer were glossy porno mags depicting duos and trios in 'hot man-to-man action!' There were no Polaroids, no letters, no receipts.

The bedside table proved no more revealing. The drawer held two paperbacks — one by John Grisham, the other by Lawrence Saunders — and a box of Kleenex.

Nothing under the bed. Not even dustballs.

I opened the closet. Shirts, suits and pants hung from the rail. Shoes lined the floor. The clothing appeared so even and regular I assumed Bill had put a finger between each item to space them properly.

The shelf above supported three cardboard boxes. I knew this was what I wanted. I took down the first one. Something shifted inside and I almost dropped it. I lowered it onto the floor without spilling the contents. I sat cross-legged beside the closet door and lifted the lid.

Inside were two photo albums, one bulging, one thin. Brown plastic, printed to look like leather, covered both. I picked the thin one first. Inside, only the first two pages had been filled; two pages of Polaroid portraits, exactly like those in the entertainment room. The rest of the leaves hadn't even been marked.

My frustration ballooned in my throat. I wanted to shout something, preferably obscene. Could one man be so fixated and so redundant? I took it personally, as though Bill was deliberately reneging on a promise.

I tossed the album towards the bed and picked up the next one. Opened it. More Polaroids.

But these ones were different. Here Bill had catalogued doorways: apartments, houses, offices, stores, steel exits. There were no dates and the times of day varied. And again I recognized some of them: a men's clothier,

a bathhouse, a cafe, a deli. All had the same distanced, documentary quality as the faces. Bill hadn't looked for the best light or the perfect angle. He'd just pressed the shutter release and gone on his way.

I started by flipping the leaves rapidly, but slowed to examine one whenever I found a familiar front. If I hadn't I would have missed Claire's store. She'd named it InDe: Interior Decor, and here it was with its white paint on the glass. An out-of-focus man leaned over a stand-up ashtray inside. The image, helped along by Jimmy Scott's fragile voice in the other room, brought a bittersweet nostalgia to me. I'd celebrated drunkenly with Claire the night she opened shop. Many times I'd brought her croissants or sandwiches on weekend afternoons. She'd introduced me to one of my boyfriends at the cash register. But also during that time a nastiness crept over her. More than once I'd asked her to stop mimicking the more effete customers; she'd treated me like a spoil sport. Our telephone conversations had grown uncomfortable because of her diatribes against her suppliers. And then her business partner, a man I'd never met, had abandoned her, declared bankruptcy for the both of them, then transferred much of the stock to another of his businesses. She'd run rabidly through every homophobic epithet I knew — queer, fairy, faggot, poof, fudge packer, bum bandit, sodomite, nancy — to describe this man. I'd finally screamed into the receiver, "Shut up! Just shut up with that shit! You're being a dumb bitch about this!" To which she replied "Then you're no better than he is, Tom. Just another two-faced cocksucker." "Better a cocksucker than a cunt," I'd spat and slammed the phone down for good.

That door stood before me again, encased in film. Bill had memorialized, maybe even fetishized it. I wanted to open the door. I wanted to hear the electronic chime as I entered. I wanted to find Claire unpacking a lamp. I wanted to talk to her. I wanted to set things right.

That desire passed quickly. Nothing could have been salvaged. I'd tried. She was too Claire. I was too Tom.

I turned the page. I scanned the pictures. There was a familiar doorway here. It led to flats above a barber shop off Parliament Street. It had been painted over many times. This is where the Recipe Man had sat so often. His absence from the picture saddened me. Of all the Polaroids in this album,

this one deserved the human connection. "Quarter please. Quarter please." I could hear him faintly, as though his voice was coming from down the hall. From the bathroom. From Bill.

I stood quickly. The album fell off my lap with a thud. Specks of white drifted and winked in my vision. I heard nothing but my own jack-hammer heart beat. And then Jimmy Scott's voice faded down at the end of another song.

I'd been holding my breath. I let it go. This stress had frayed my nerves. Hallucinating. Me, actually hallucinating. The perfect kind too; they taught us in Psych 101 that auditory hallucinations were the first signs of schizophrenia. Claire had taken that course with me, and when we'd heard this I'd whispered in her ear, "Sam I am. Kill your neighbours. Bow wow. Woof woof." She'd brayed with laughter, earning us disdain from the prof and his T.A.'s. I could remember that year quite clearly. We had escaped from our families, transferred to another city, found release. It was during the same Psych class we'd heard the term 'closure': the mind's ability to fill in what cannot be seen. The prof had given the example of walking down a street and knowing where you've been without turning around. Between Claire and I closure became the word to substitute I love you. I told her, "We've known each other so long, we can rely on closure. We don't have to haul out the past and examine it. We share the same path. We share the same history. And that sort of bond is ... is love." I meant it. We weren't lovers, and wouldn't be, but we did love each other.

And now, if Claire ever thought of me, we would still have the same history. We'd experienced the same events from our different perspectives, never too disparate except at the end. Claire'd had her back to mine. She had been unable to turn around, paralyzed by misfortune. And I still couldn't forgive her.

I picked the album up from the floor. I closed it and put it back in the box. I placed its companion in there too. I lifted the box back to its original spot.

Did I need to look in the other boxes? I wasn't sure I did. I'd probably find more books of Polaroids. I thought I'd seen enough. Maybe Bill had been unable to form a closure in his mind. Or maybe he was afraid of an inability to do it. My theory was, he had to record his encounters, his routines,

just in case he forgot. A couple of pieces that Claire had sold stood downstairs. He'd probably been a customer and had to photograph the occasion. Maybe he'd seen the Recipe Man often enough too. How he took the picture I don't know, but chances were he paid cash. And for what? A reminder of someone's hurting life? I don't think Bill took his subjects too much into consideration. Bill was photographing Bill's life; the albums were a map of his movements and interactions.

Thank the lord for Psych 101 when you're snooping through a dead man's belongings.

I started to close the closet door, when I thought, what the hell. There's no such thing as too much cartography. I pulled the second box down, set it on the floor and opened it.

No albums this time. Instead I found a thick pack of folders. Bill had marked each with a title: The Top Shelf, Renew Refinishing, Exile Designs, Everything, Diary Antiques. But in the middle of them, one caught my attention with such harsh possessiveness I couldn't move. InDe: Interior Decor.

I pulled the folder out slowly. I opened it.

The first loose sheet was a contract, the second a bank loan, the third a lease, the rest invoices. Two signatures graced the bottom of each page. Claire's and Bill's.

I laughed. It came out of me suddenly. My shoulders hitched, I hiccupped, and the air stuttered through my throat. A lightness touched the top of my head. I gripped the folder so I wouldn't drop it. The connection, the discovery, made me giddy. Dizzy. My laughter grew out of control. I fell onto my side. The papers spilled all across the floor. Somehow even this litter was funny.

It seemed both terrible and apt that my night would end this way: out of the past had come a ghost, shaking its chains pathetically. I laughed until tears wet the floor beneath my cheek. Claire's ex-business partner sat dead on the toilet in the other room. I'd used him to gain an experience, to create a new and unique memory. No Polaroids of the mundane for me. I knew Claire wouldn't need pictures to remind herself of encounters with him either. From whatever pain Bill had caused Claire at that time, from whatever epithets Claire and I had hurled at each other to end our

friendship, from whatever stress the man had visited on both of us, I was glad to be here now. I was happy to have seen the Polaroids and business files. It lightened my heart to be lying here, giggling sporadically now, in the midst of the papers.

I wanted to share this with Claire. I could call her up to tell her everything from the pick-up to the files. But I knew I wouldn't. And because I knew I wouldn't, I stopped laughing.

I slowly stood. I looked around me at the clean, uncluttered room. At the open cardboard box. At the light down the hall from the entertainment room. And I wept.

⁊⁘

It wasn't a long walk to the Yonge Street subway line. The snow still flocked the side-street curbs, undisturbed. Multicoloured Christmas lights cast splotched prisms on the bright ground. Bill's Polaroid camera hung from my neck.

At the townhouse, the bedroom remained as I'd found it: closet door closed, boxes packed and stored on the top shelf. The CDs rested side by side in alphabetical order, Bill Evans and Jimmy Scott both in their places. The stereo was off. The lights in the entertainment room were off. My scotch glass stood clean, in the kitchen cupboard with six other tumblers just like it. Bill sat on the toilet, pants around his ankles, illuminated by the harsh fluorescents and reflective tiles. Rigor mortis settled in his muscles. The house, really, was lifeless.

They'd locked the subway doors. I'd forgotten the time. No matter, I could always take the 24-hour drunk bus. There was a stop right here. But first I had to use the phone.

I got into the phone booth on the street corner. I picked up the receiver. Could I really do this? "One, two, three," I said aloud, then punched 9-1-1.

It rang three times. "Emergency," a crisp female voice said.

"There's a dead guy. In a house." I spoke rapidly. They taped these things. They could play it back. I knew because I'd seen it on television. I gave the address. "It was natural. Maybe a heart attack or an aneurysm or

something, I don't know. I tried mouth-to-mouth. Really. I tried. I tried to save him. He's on the second floor. You'll know because there's a light on."

"Okay. It's alright. Could you tell me your — "

I hung up. My palms felt cold and damp. I left the phone booth and stood at the bus stop. I realized they could also trace the call to this location and have a squad car here in minutes. My bowels turned to ice. Shit. Frozen shit.

I scanned the street for taxis. A Hyundai sped north. I clenched my fists, fingernails biting into the heels of my palms. I was preparing myself for imminent arrest and questioning when my salvation came into view: the drunk bus, the vomit express, its blue beacon announcing its all-night, all-morning status. I looked for cop cars. None.

The bus stopped in front of me. I boarded. The driver, a moustached man not much older than myself, gave me a clipped but friendly "Good evening." I walked down the aisle to the back seats. I didn't see any flashing lights outside on the street. Two women, the only other passengers, sat by the rear doors. They wore their hair short and their faces without the mask of makeup. Their leather jackets covered warm sweaters.

The women confirmed my suspicions when one leaned her head on the other's shoulder and her companion stroked her hair. Their faces tilted towards each other and they kissed.

I, for one, enjoy public displays of affection, especially between gays and lesbians. It leaves me with the haunting illusion that by persistence these actions can save us from heterosexual bigotry.

In mid-kiss, one of them looked back. "Hey, there," she said warmly. "You with the camera. Hey there." She waved.

Her girlfriend turned. "A Polaroid. Right on!"

"Take our picture," both said at once. They laughed at their synchronicity.

I smiled. "You really want me to?"

"Yeah, yeah."

"We're asking, right?"

"Alright." I stood and sat in the seat opposite them. The vinyl covering had the graffiti *L.B. & J.F. 4ever!* scratched in it with ballpoint. "Just one," I

asked, "or do you maybe want two?"

"One!"

"One for all and all for one!"

I raised the camera to my eye. With that action they shifted to face me, back to window, back on breasts. Arms came down, went up. They nestled with such enthusiasm I knew they couldn't be drunk on anything but each other. When their contentment had peaked, I pressed the shutter release. The flash blazed. The motor wound. The camera ejected its square.

The woman with her back to the window looked right at me and said "You are beautiful. Sincerely."

"Thanks."

"You remind me so much of the first girl I ever fell in love with."

"Hey!" her girlfriend said with mock-jealousy.

I smiled. "All us queers look alike."

They laughed and I handed them the picture.

ૐ

When Claire and Tom were in their last year of high school, a second-hand clothing store opened not far from the school property. That autumn they began to go there twice a week. They each accumulated impressive vintage wardrobes. Guy, the owner, a sharply handsome man in his 30s, recognized in them an eccentricity frowned upon by their peers. But he fostered it. "Claire, I've got this '50s' skirt that dances like you walk," or "Try this blazer, Tom, it's as duke as you are." They began to feel good about themselves as they never had in years. In Tom he recognized something else.

They increased their trips to the store. By winter they visited Guy more than they shopped. Claire and Tom always went together, but one afternoon Tom set out on his own. He had a spare. Claire didn't. He told himself he was going to buy a shirt, but consumerism was not the true motive.

Tom had a crush on Guy; an awed, trembling, school-boy crush, and the older man knew it. Guy fueled it when he winked at Tom after some joke, or when he patted his shoulders to fit a jacket, or when he insisted on putting a tie around the boy's neck and knotting it himself.

Tom was the only customer that afternoon. They talked lightly on current events, Tom's classes and Guy's inventory. The youth's voice rose questioningly at the end of every sentence, though he asked no questions. Finally Guy said, "I should take a break." Before Tom could say goodbye and see you, Guy was locking the front door. "Would you like some tea?" he asked. "Come into the back."

Weak bulbs illuminated the stock room. Guy had stacked boxes on shelves and labelled them. Shirts and jackets hung awaiting pricing. Two easy chairs stood by a side table. This was where they'd have tea.

Guy kissed Tom first. It surprised the boy. He'd hoped for it, but hadn't expected. He stiffened, but soon relaxed into the other's lips. Guy released him and whispered, "I've been waiting to get you back here."

Here was where they'd have tea, but later, days later. This day Tom lost what he thought of as his virginity. The clearest feeling from that afternoon was one of both foreignness and familiarity. Tom held another man's cock in his hand; a cock like his own; a cock not like his own. Guy did the rest. As soon as Tom came he was flushed with shame and guilt. It mortified him when Guy rubbed his face across his belly, breathing deeply.

Tom stood and pulled on his underwear and pants. His shirt hung crumpled in his hand as he stammered, "I've got to get back to class. I've already cut physics."

"It's okay, Tom," Guy said patiently. "It's okay."

The rest of the afternoon and evening, and even that night climbing into bed, Tom could smell Guy on him. He didn't understand how he could be so elated and terrified at the same time.

Tom began visiting Guy twice as often: by himself, for sex, and with Claire, who didn't know, for clothes. The shopping trips were fraught with tension, but Guy understood. He lavished so much attention on Claire that she didn't notice. If Tom met him after work, Guy and the boy would have long post-coital conversations, sipping tea or coffee. Guy gave comfort and advice, letting him know he was a mentor, not a lover.

One afternoon that spring, Guy flipped over the closed sign and unlocked the door. He squeezed Tom's arm. "See you with Claire," he said.

Tom left grinning. He took two steps and found Claire seated just inside the gravel alley beside the store, her back to the brick.

"Claire!" he almost shouted.

She looked up and shielded her eyes against the sun. "Hi Tom. You just with Guy?"

"Uh, yeah. He took a break. We had tea."

She stood. "Uh-huh."

"Do you want to go in?"

"Nah. I cut gym, so I may as well make physics." They walked slowly back toward the school. Claire had her hands in her coat pockets with her head cast down. "Guy's kind of cute, don't you think?" She didn't sound rhetorical.

"Well, I guess so. Yeah."

They continued walking in silence. At the track field she said, "Tom...?" A question was forming, but then she wrinkled her brow and didn't say any more.

MEMORIES _of_ BEEF

written by margaret webb
designed by peter mansour

Bad Egg

strange goings on at the neighbour's place, a riderless horse tells me

they're taking in strays, cats and dogs even homeless people too
the barn's got beds and 100 boxes of eggs to grade before we
get through the door to sleep

but the eggs are human I tell you

throwing one against the wall strands of hair and tendons like cooked
spaghetti stick in the white

piss on your human eggs they say you're going to grade them for sale

and who am I to say what's not chicken?

my mother wears high heel shoes strapped to her cowboy boots and
my accountant father would seduce me except I ran
when he tattooed his bald head blue

and my mother is leading the riderless horse up the lane down

doesn't yet know her daughter's bought it behind the barn sniffing glue

Memories of Beef

"The female sex organs are the blind spot."
— Jane Gallop

"I think where I am not, therefore I am where I think not."
— Jacques Lacan

1.
seven o'clock and the vet wants to go
home to his steak and his wife but
he's got his arm to his shoulder up the ass
of a cow yanking the calf
out by its hind legs already 100
pounds too big to walk even jerkily the way new calves do and blind

steam from the manure
steam from the afterbirth
steam from the uterus that's come out
with the calf

2.
in Montreal, where memory is
occurring, metaphor leaps over whole
decades of my life with slant
regard to metonymy, what simmers beneath
the surface and connects me

oh, I buy *The Gazette*, get groceries, go to the bank
but what I'm saying is
I don't go out in the city

3.
I'm 12 and watching this cow
having been fed to make beef
too fat to have calves
its calf too big to stand
my father says
go to the house already
an hour ago

the cow never getting up the next day
becomes string-wrapped
packages in our freezer

in the summer it's my job
to wash the grey liquid oozing
from the blind calf's eyes
to keep flies off

4.
I don't know why I'm having this memory of beef
I stopped eating it months ago
maybe I'm anemic; I sleep too much
last night I went to bed at 11 woke up
at 3 went back to sleep
at 6 got up at 10
face of the clock ticking a kind of metonymy
relating what passes
for days, lying
in the heat watching flies
mate on the ceiling
too lazy to get up
to close the screen

you think I'm depressed
on account of the sleep
on account of not going out in the city
on account of watching the flies

my father scraped the uterus up with a shovel

not that I want a connection
between that uterus and my
not going out in the city

I'm not trying to make one
I'm trying to make a poem

what the flies are doing here I don't know

5.
I am writing the poem because I believe a poem can

a) soak up the excess of metaphor
b) supply memory with its own metonymy
c) release me from trying to bend not just lines but the whole
   of my being into its absurd connections and
d) give me my life back

when I think in metaphor there is
a certain rhythm which does not let me change
direction seemingly changes
of its own volition leaping
over logic to create another kind
of logic which makes street corners
hazardous keeping me
indoors and dreaming
a fatted farmer birthing an anorexic
calf and a fence I'm trying to jump over
which is too

high or a man and a woman who have invited me to dinner when I
would still go out in the city but they discover that I have these memories of beef and then pretend not to have invited me to dinner, saying
there is no roast in the oven and the table is set for their inlaws whom
I wouldn't like any more than the beef

6.
it was after dinner that I dreamt
the fatted farmer giving birth to the anorexic
calf though it came out
the other way around

there might be a connection
in the breech
if you don't fill in the other

connections, it was Freud who said you need
the blind spots to see

how the flies squeeze black body to black body
over the face of the blind calf
to drink the liquid from the blind calf's eyes

and the calf not having a mother

7.
that relation being another kind of metonymy
the umbilical cord of metonymy
that is cut

turning the mother into a free-floating signifier
or three-quarter-inch
steaks in the deep freeze

turning metaphor into a schizophrenic leaping
on young calf's legs

8.
in the city that I don't go out in
there's a bar that I don't go into
riding my bicycle one day
(in a time I used to go out)
it caught my attention
that bar being a lesbian bar I lost
sight of the straightness
of the road I hit the curb I flew forward
and jammed my pelvis
when I hit the curb

it wasn't that my uterus had to be
scraped up off the street
only that it felt that way

9.
my other cow memory is of selling that calf at the end of
summer I got $100 for wiping the goo off its face for three months
I got new clothes for school in the fall it went to the slaughterhouse

The Dream is Woman

No, the buzzer is not dreamt
but the dream is woman
getting up to answer the door
to a stranger naked to her skin
she lets him in...

confesses
trying on sixteen dresses during
her lunch hour without any panties on
she wanted to see which ones showed
pubic hair just a hint
of dark shadow she said

confessing
that she never left the office that day
wouldn't even try on new underwear
without first covering the crotch
with Saran Wrap she had
six carrot sticks, celery,
one percent cottage cheese on
melba toast and spent the rest
of her lunch hour applying
nail polish to the run
in her stocking to stop
stop stop talking
she thinks touch me
why don't you touch me
if you could lick here

you could put a finger there
the point where he's fading
faster she talks faster
can't hold him in
says what is the matter
you're not a cunt man?
yells fag fag as he flees
down the hallway
leading out of her dream
which isn't anymore
but the buzzer still is

reaching for the alarm
she says open the fucking door
– to herself

Spring Summer Fall

1.
We were making love in the wading pool at Parc Lafontaine
and you were so far inside me I wondered
what power you possessed
to keep going

and then it broke off

your penis like stone from the statue of a Greek god
or missing appendage on a Ken doll

surprised more than alarmed, the shock
nothingness gave us, the self
consciousness of your hand
drifting over your absence

but I became Venus eager for that eel of delight squirting
from our grasping hands, splashing in the pond and laughing like it
was some love game still —

but I was thinking, if I got it for myself would I
then need you?

and you sensed the leaves had changed the surface of the pond
was red and gold clouding over with feathers from migrating geese
and ducks alighting

it wasn't summer anymore

and the cold made your teeth chatter so hard your eyes went blank
and your hair hung in thick rope strands making you forlorn
as a statue in a park that birds land on

2.
though I had found your penis

I couldn't bring myself to tell you

or give it back

I was so hungry

3.
I bought popcorn

I fed it to the birds

The Visit

when I stepped into the doctor's office, she was old and I was young
but she had a head full of red curls

red wonderful curls

I had a woman's problem

I had desire
for a woman

she put her stethoscope on the heart of the problem, the lethargy
of skin grown thick over my soul

and in the light of that knowing she grew younger

and younger

the wrinkles on her face melting into skin so smooth

so smooth I could just reach out and touch those curls
if I could just reach out and touch my desire roused
to the white wonder of two firm breasts at mouth level
talking to me

a tongue depressor in her hand

she said open your mouth and I did and I did close it over a nipple
then the whole of her breast pressing to the back of my throat

I said *ahhhh*

she seemed satisfied

I Dream Your Hand

suddenly aware of the skin
between souls
after late-night
conversation blurring
a question
of

another glass of red wine or
the fire dying
down or if I dream
your hand
reaches in to
pull me from bed
and I take you
in like this is
what you wanted
lip on breast sucking
nipple tongue there
there
awake
you are
in the next
room and
know nothing
of my dream

or do
you

stop where
do friends stop
being and skin
begin —

If My Poem Were A Bottle of Red Wine

1.
while other girls wore tight jeans to school dances and stuffed
Kleenex into bras because the fashion then was to have breasts I was
writing poetry and dreaming about meeting Leonard Cohen
in a Montreal coffee house

my intentions were

not all pure

poetry being as good a container for desire as tight jeans so I
thought then by the time I looked up from my notebook
I was 18 and still virginal

despite my professional aspirations

I gave up poetry

tried marriage anxious for a decent interval of contraceptive sex but
my biological clock started ticking it was a manicured fingernail
tapping against a bottle of red wine

a single key clacking on an old Underwood typewriter

n n n n

we slept as two fertile souls for two weeks before I managed to strike

ow

popping the cork I honestly expected red wine to come gushing out

not my soul

which my legalized lover found sticky preferring containers that shape
words into oh-so-nice form like lips smacking around a bottle but

my mind pours over which is not good for marriage

or the suburbs

2.
when I moved to Montreal I swear it was the poetics of coincidence
that I managed to squeeze seven I's into this sentence on the same day
I discovered my new place was one block from Len's but secretly I
thought the grammar of my fate had been genetically encoded though
I don't believe that kind of confidence becomes a female poet

sometimes I see Len sitting on his front step when he's not licking red
wine off Suzanne's back or downing caffeine at the Bagel Cafe

to ease into a rhythmic mood

I write poetry my editor says he can psycho-analyze

take it to my shrink thinking I might save some money but she says
she can't psycho-analyze poetry though maybe she's just not good with
poetic device actually asks what that sticky pathetic fallacy is doing

poking out at odd angles

and did it have something to do with the humidity in Montreal?

3.
or envy

that I have divorced my body's obedience to conjugal convention
lets me have a casual lover now

in the stink hot of July nights we sit in the park in front of Len's house
fantasizing about the words he might be tracing in the sweat
of Suzanne's back

I don't tell my lover I write poetry

he might expect a dedication

want me to move down to the river drip desire over his body lick it off
all night long write ballads that would uncasualize my love he doesn't
understand the slavery of sentences like Len does I have a sentence of
humour to maintain on top of strict form that keeps my sentences
from breaking out of control shit like this the critics say women
writers have no control over our sentences give us an inch of white
space and we charge off like a bunch of lesbians forgetting who
invented the line that proper restraint would keep our looser halves
from violating poetry with repetitive multiple orgasms repetitive
multiple orgasms taste sweet as spilled wine to my lips but

are perhaps a little exhausting for critics or tongues of lovers of poets
who write personally not writing about him is the only way I can keep
the whole affair from getting too sticky

because he wouldn't like my poetry then

4.

meanwhile the sentences of my poems get longer and longer trying to wrap their syntax around big concepts like universality and narrative construct that push my sticky emotion and confessional lust to the very margin

to make room for Suzanne?

meanwhile the sentences of my poems get longer and longer trying to mop up the spillage

5.

I have tried to make my poem into the shape of a bottle of red wine

maybe if I go back to the girls in the tight jeans alternating sucks on a bottle of red wine with their boyfriends

teasing the shape of their tissued breasts

it would seem more finished that way

When All She Intended Was Blue Sky

13 and I am

kissing a girl in the backseat of my father's car

either I am pretending she is a guy or I am a guy

either way

it's not lesbian

because of the pretending

*

the first time I met him I seduced him

or at least if we looked back and had to say

who seduced whom

we would have to say it was me because I kissed him first
then he kissed me

then we were just tongues inside each other's mouths

*

he being an Arab Jew

is what I like about him

that he doesn't fit inside

any borders

he has parties

inviting his Jewish friends and his Arab friends and I end up fighting
with them in the kitchen about which part of him they don't like

defending the other part at the same time not liking the part of him
I am fighting with at that moment

we argue like this for hours not giving a single thought to how many
fights like this occur in kitchens

*

after she gets to know him

the she being me I am

talking in the third person

because it seems more

appropriate at this moment

the girl from the back seat showing up in my life

at the oddest of moments

*

I have been turned down for a part in a play but
I have the lines so I say them anyway

and she is the only person in the audience

or a lump has been removed from my breast

I am lying in a hospital bed and she is lying beside me

she has also had a lump removed from her breast

the doctor says our lumps are benign

but they are missing to us anyway

*

standing in a bookstore on Sunday afternoon she realizes
she hates poetry

after writing poetry for 20 years suddenly
every bright flip of metaphor grates on her nerves like sunshine

outside when she's inside
writing
wanting to be outside
drinking wine at the cafe across the street
a glass of white wine
a cool glass of dry white wine

*

when you realize there is a rhythm in poetry
stress, repetition, cadence
careful-
ly measured
out so you can't
break out you can
argue about it in the kitchen
strain against it even as it inserts
a child into your life a house with a backyard
when all you intended was blue sky

*

another time the girl from the back seat and I are sitting with a group
of girls under a tree in a meadow
we are older so the thickening of skin on our chests
is thicker
and some of us are pretending to be guys and the rest of us are
pretending to be girls
either way
because of the pretending
it's not lesbian

*

after this she grew up

after this she fell in love with her Arab-Jewish boyfriend
and got married

after this she started running into the girl from the back seat of the car
at the oddest of moments

*

sometimes she can't stop

writing about herself

in the third person

*

if she writes about herself

in the second person

she would have to tell herself

things she does not want to hear

*

when you make love with your husband

you fantasize that you are

with the girl from the backseat of the car

you being second-person plural

so there is no question that the two of you are making love

and not masturbating

*

you go to a play with your husband and discover it was written
by the girl from the back seat of the car

the girl being a woman now

the play having occurred before the lumps were removed
from your breasts

in the play two women are lying in bed dying and the doctor says
they are dying so the audience knows they are dying and your husband
leans over and whispers, "Christ, they are dying"

even though the two women are in bed, lying
together, clinging together

there is no question the scene is not lesbian

because of the dying

*

it is a play in which the actors forget one or two of the lines

after the author says, "whole chunks of text went missing"

but the play closes in around the space and the audience does not
notice the space

after a while the author doesn't notice either

*

even without constructing a story this is what happens

*

after I decide that I hate poetry I find myself

in the kitchen at a party talking to someone

who says poetry is like wallpaper

I spend the whole party in the kitchen

arguing the merits of poetry

arguing with him even as he is leaving

all the way down the hallway and into the elevator

until I can see he is afraid

I will follow him home

*

you have to be pulled out of the elevator by your Arab-Jewish husband who wants to be friends with everyone

*

I am not able to dissect which part of me is Arab and which part is Jewish

my psychiatrist says that my being woman and lesbian makes it an interesting theoretical question, but how could you know anyway?

*

after the play I have a reunion with the playwright who used to be the girl from the back seat of the car

we hug to say hello then we hug to say goodbye

in between we get each other glasses of wine because it is opening night and there is free wine

after we walk each other to the door because the reception is over

and in that space she says

I have always been attracted to you

and I say

I have always been attracted to you

and then we say goodbye because the reception is over

the front door of the theatre closing over these two lines of text

*

being in the second-person might make you wonder

why did the author simply not create a character who would run back into the theatre and retrieve those two lines?

*

if you went running back and she wasn't there
where would the story be then

*

her Arab-Jewish husband touches her arm and opens the door of the taxi
moments before he had raised his arm and hailed the taxi
she wonders how many times he has come running after her
how certain he must be of her reality

*

she has walked past the theatre many times since
and it has always been there

*

considering the reality of the poem, it becomes impossible
to analyze
the Arab-Jewishness of her husband
the girl from the back seat of a car
a woman named by pronouns
you wonder if what will appear is a house with a backyard
when all she intended was blue sky

*

you wonder if she can go back to that moment with the girl
in the back seat of the car
without pretending this time
you wonder if her life is pretending now and if that pretending then
was the only thing real

the present having closed over the past where she was not acting
but pretending

the past acting to become present acting to become future

you could pretend that none of this is happening to you

*

in the bookstore she turns the page of the book she is reading
when she comes to the very last word on the page

*

I wasn't conscious at all of speaking missing lines

we had been practising all our lives

to say this

and to say this

*

sitting in the cafe

drinking a glass of wine

the taste of letting go, into

*

the strain of holding the girl from the back seat of the car

all my life

at a distance

making my life in that distance

*

when she stands outside theatres

her Arab-Jewish husband orders them taxis and taxis continue
to respond

so that she can hardly doubt their reality here

the comfortable parts of their lives filling in like props

the house, the backyard, the children

to make props lie flat on the stage you must cut off their ragged bottoms

who is he ordering taxis for

*

when I imagine a life with this girl from the back seat of the car

shopping lists are left on scraps of paper
on the fridge door

which seems more real than the note I leave her after the first night
we spend together:

I slept with
slept with a woman
a woman I love
her breast
warm
in my mouth
girl
girl

and after

the way the morning sun makes a pattern on the floor
I'm not sure how she'll read it

whether she'll interpret it as a sign to bring groceries back from the store

or whether I'll be there when she gets back

and whether she is

or I am

and this is

tentative

I imagine

we will start leaving notes like this

Other titles from Insomniac Press:

Beds & Shotguns
by Diana Fitzgerald Bryden, Paul Howell McCafferty, Tricia Postle, and Death Waits

Beds & Shotguns is a metaphor for the extremes of love. It is also a collection by four emerging poets who write about the gamut of experiences between these opposites from romantic to obsessive, fantastic to possessive. These poems and stories capture love in its broadest meanings and are set in a dynamic, lyrical landscape.
5 1/4" x 8 1/4" • 96 pages • trade paperback • isbn 1-895837-28-6 • $13.99

Playing in the Asphalt Garden
by Phlip Arima, Jill Battson, Tatiana Freire-Lizama, and Stan Rogal

This book features new Canadian urban writers, who express the urban experience — not the city of buildings and streets, but as a concentration of human experience, where a rapid and voluminous exchange of ideas, messages, power and beliefs takes place.
5 3/4" x 9" • 128 pages • trade paperback • isbn 1-895837-20-0 • $14.99

Mad Angels and Amphetamines
by Nik Beat, Mary Elizabeth Grace, Noah Leznoff, and Matthew Remski

A collection by four emerging Canadian writers and three graphic designers. In this book, design is an integral part of the prose and poetry. Each writer collaborated with a designer so that the graphic design is an interpretation of the writer's works. Nik Beat's lyrical and unpretentious poetry; Noah Leznoff's darkly humourous prose and narrative poetic cycles; Mary Elizabeth Grace's Celtic dialogues and mystical images; and Matthew Remski's medieval symbols and surrealistic style of story; this is the mixture of styles that weave together in *Mad Angels and Amphetamines*.
6" x 9" • 96 pages • trade paperback • isbn 1-895837-14-6 • $12.95

Insomniac Press • 378 Delaware Ave. • Toronto, ON, Canada • M6H 2T8
phone: (416) 538-4308 • fax: (416) 596-6743